Double-Click for Trouble

Chris Woodworth

DOUBLE-CLICK FOR TROUBLE

FARRAR, STRAUS AND GIROUX
NEW YORK

This is a work of fiction. All of the characters, organizations, locales, and events portrayed in this novel are products of the author's imagination or are used fictitiously, and any similarities to real life persons or locales are unintended and entirely coincidental.

www.fsgkidsbooks.com

Library of Congress Cataloging-in-Publication Data
Woodworth, Chris, date.
    Double click for trouble / Chris Woodworth.— 1st ed.
        p. cm.
    Summary: After he is caught viewing inappropriate websites on the
Internet, a fatherless, thirteen-year-old Chicago boy is sent to rural Indiana
to spend school break with his eccentric great-uncle.
    ISBN-13: 978-0-374-30987-9
    ISBN-10: 0-374-30987-6
    [1. Great-uncles—Fiction. 2. Fathers—Fiction. 3. Country life—
Fiction. 4. Coming of age—Fiction.] I. Title.

PZ7.W8794Bu 2008
[Fic]—dc22

                                                              2006038351

For Jane,
my mother-in-law and friend

Double-Click for Trouble

$$\boxed{1}$$

At night I pull my blanket over my head. It blocks out the clickety sound of Mom's computer, as well as the light that sneaks in around the window blind. It was my favorite way to fall asleep until Mr. Black, my science teacher, taught us about how expelling carbon dioxide can make you sleepy. He says that too much can kill you. I didn't die from it before I learned that, but now, no matter how good I feel under that blanket, I start thinking about breathing used-up air. Next thing I know, I'm yanking off the covers, gasping.

Mr. Black ruined one of my joys in life, is how I see it.

Like tonight. I almost drift off, then remember that I'm breathing poison. I throw back the blanket, and cool air fans across my face, getting me good and awake. I open the door and look out into the living room. Mom is bent over her computer keyboard. Her long hair, blond like mine, is pulled back into a ponytail.

Mom works at the Chicago Hilltop Hotel, at their coffee

bar called Riverside Room. She has to get up super early and take a bus across town so she can smile and make sure the guests' days get off to a good start with a cappuccino or latte. All they have to do is roll out of bed and take an elevator downstairs, no smiles required. Then Mom takes a college class in the afternoons, comes home, and takes more online. She always stays up late working on her homework.

Homework is another joy-killer in my life. But I don't just hate my own. I hate seeing Mom so stressed out over hers. Like now, hunched over the computer when she should be resting.

I ease my door open and our cat, Princess, slinks around the corner and jumps onto the windowsill. I walk Comanche-style, toe-heel-toe-heel, so Mom won't hear me. Princess watches my every move but sits like a statue. For once I'm glad she's a cat, and not the dog I'd rather have. Sidestepping the loose floorboard beside the end table, I sneak up behind Mom, gently take the tip of her ponytail, and tickle the back of her neck. She jumps a foot.

"Eddie McCall! You know that annoys me!" She spins around in her desk chair. "Why aren't you asleep?"

"It's Mr. Black's fault," I say.

Her frown changes into that look of concern she gets. "Oh, Eddie, don't tell me you're having trouble in science."

I grab the Rubik's Cube she's had since the eighties off her desk and twist it. "Mom, please. Not the 'school is important' lecture again. And, no, I'm not having trouble."

She takes the puzzle from my hand. "Are you sure?"

Then I remember that progress reports come out soon.

"Not that I know of," I add, just in case. I go to the fridge, pull the handle, and grab the carton of milk.

"Then what is it?"

"It's hard to sleep with all that typing. Besides, you're always tired, Mom. Why don't you give it a rest?"

She reaches for her ponytail, pulls off the thing that looks like a scrunched-up snake, and runs her hands through her hair. You'd think her hair is her favorite toy, the way she puts it up and takes it down about a gazillion times a day.

"Eddie, I'm sorry." She comes over and takes two glasses out of the cabinet. "But when am I supposed to do my homework?"

"You could let me type it for you." Typing is the only thing Mom allows me to do on the computer. And only when she's home.

"Or let me do research for you on the Internet." I smile at her, trying to copy the picture she framed of me as a kindergartner, even though I've had seven more school pictures taken since. It's the one with the smile that she says melts her heart.

"Nice try," she says, heart frozen solid.

I sigh. There's no competing with a wide-eyed, toothless smile when your permanent teeth came in three sizes too big.

I don't think Mom's typing at night would bother me nearly as much if she would let me surf the Net. I have computer-envy. Now, there's an expanded vocabulary word. I'll have to use it on Mrs. Cabot, my English teacher.

I try again. "Mom, other kids go online. It's not like I'd go to any Web sites you wouldn't want me to." I don't make eye contact on that one.

"It's not just that, young man. With two of my classes online, I don't know how I'd keep up my schedule if the computer got a virus."

"Haven't you heard of antivirus software?"

"I have that, Eddie. Still, you can't be too careful. The computer is a gift from Uncle Peavey. A very *generous* gift that I could never replace."

Mom's uncle, Peavey, is the only relative she has now besides me. He comes at Christmastime bearing gifts, but that's his only resemblance to Santa. Thin and short, he looks more like a shy elf. Still, I want to say if he can afford one computer, he can probably afford another, but I don't think I'd score any points with that.

Mom pours milk into the glasses. "You think the computer drives *you* crazy? You should see what it does to me. If I don't have my work done, it's almost like a person sitting there glaring at me. It won't let me go to sleep until my work is finished."

I take the glass she offers and feel bad. We live in a small apartment. Mom gave me the only bedroom, which means she sleeps on the pull-out sofa. The milk doesn't taste so good, but I make myself drink it. I don't want it to go to waste, because bedrooms aren't the only thing we're short on. We don't have a lot of money, either.

"Sorry, Mom," I say as I head back to bed. Tomorrow I'm going to look up *sorry* in the thesaurus during English class.

It's the word that I need to expand in my vocabulary, since it's definitely the one I use the most.

Next morning the buzzing from the alarm clock feels like a drill working its way through my brain. I hit the top of the clock to shut it off and throw back the covers. If I stay warm, I know I'll go back to sleep.

I step into my jeans and pull on my orange T-shirt that says PROPERTY OF CHICAGO CORRECTIONAL FACILITIES. I saved my allowance for three weeks to buy it at one of the stores on Navy Pier. When Mom saw it, she rolled her eyes and said, "Please, God, let this not be a sign of things to come." It's my favorite.

Every morning Mom hangs a note on the medicine cabinet before she goes to work: it says "Brush teeth and use deodorant!" I rip it off, wad it, and shoot it into the trash. She treats me like a baby, but I don't say anything because I know she feels bad that she isn't here when I get ready for school.

Mom used to work as a hostess for a restaurant. When dinner was ready at home, she'd pretend I was a customer. "This way, sir. Please watch your step, sir." Then she'd put a folded paper in my hand like a menu. Inside she'd have drawn a burger or whatever we were going to eat, because I wasn't old enough to read. But that was when Mrs. McIntosh lived upstairs and babysat me. Now our neighbors are the Sweeneys, and Mom changed jobs so she could be home with me after school.

I check Princess's water dish, snatch a Pop-Tart, and lock up. In the hall I grab my basketball. Nothing gets my day off to a better start than to shoot a few before the bus comes. I pull down the basketball hoop that's attached to the front of the building, stash my book bag, and lose myself to the rhythm. Just the ball, the rim, and me. Perfect.

I make my third basket out of three when the door opens and out blasts my best friend, Jared Sweeney. His brown hair looks black because it's still wet. Jared's motto is "Dad can force me to wash, but he can't force me to be neat." And it's true. He shampoos but draws the line at combing.

"Yo!" I yell, but he doesn't hear me with earbuds glued to his head. I chuck the ball at him to get his attention. He must have seen it out of the corner of his eye and catches it. He has great reflexes.

"Nice try," he says about my aborted attempt to hit him with the ball. He dribbles it to the beat of his iPod back to the front door, tosses it into our building, then stands beside me to wait for the bus.

It's great living in the same apartment building as my best friend. Jared's the kind of guy I'd like to be. He's funny, awesome at sports, and has so much. Mom says his divorced parents are both trying to buy his love. I wish she could afford to buy mine.

The only thing I have that Jared doesn't is a full-time mom. He lives with his dad. His mom lives in another state, so she just visits. At least Jared has a dad; I don't.

Well, I suppose I have a dad, but I've never seen him. I must have his eyes, though, because mine are blue and Mom's and Uncle Peavey's are brown. Mom gets agitated when I ask about him, so I back off. Sometimes I think she doesn't let me have access to the Internet because she's afraid I'll find him. You read about that stuff all the time. People who are adopted find their birth parents online. And I'm not saying that thought hasn't crossed my mind, but how can you find a person when you don't even know his name?

Maybe someday she'll tell me. I think she worries I might care that she never married my dad, but that's not the problem. I wish there was a man around to answer the kind of questions I can't ask Mom. She doesn't have any brothers or sisters. My grandma died before I was born, and my grandpa passed away when I was four. That leaves just my great-uncle Peavey, my grandpa's brother. I guess I know him a little, but we're not what you'd call tight. Plus, he's so shy he doesn't exactly invite questions.

"Only three more days, Eddie," Jared says to me.

"Three days, Whip." I call him by his nickname. We both go to Randolph Middle School, a year-round school, which isn't as bad as it sounds. We go to school on a twelve-week track, get four off for vacation, go twelve, get off four, and so on for the whole year. We only have three more days until the next vacation. Whip counts down every day, even if it's the first day of the track.

Although we've both just been promoted to eighth grade, we don't share the same classes. Two years ago, the school did testing and put me into the Advanced Placement Program. When I got bumped up, Jared called me "The Professor." I loved it. Not the name, especially, but you feel like you belong when someone gives you a nickname. Jared puts Miracle Whip on everything he eats, so I call him Whip. He soon lost interest and went back to my name, but I still call him Whip, secretly wishing he cared enough to call me by a nickname, too.

Mom was thrilled when the teachers told her they thought I was so smart I'd get bored, and they wanted me to be challenged. All that means is I have to work twice as hard now, while Whip gets to sing jingles like "Verbs are something you do-do-do." I have Dragon-Breath Mrs. Cabot urging me to "expand my vocabulary," and I don't get to be in any classes with Whip.

"It's good to get a little distance, Eddie," Mom said. "You live in the same building and can see him all the time, anyway."

What she really meant was she doesn't like him. I can tell by the way her voice gets sharper and her answers shorter when I talk about him. Kind of like she gets when I ask about my dad. If I question why she doesn't like Whip, she says things like "I like him, it's just that he's *unsupervised*." It's no more Whip's fault he doesn't have a mom than it's my fault I don't have a dad. I don't tell her that, though, because I value my life.

The school bus pulls up and Whip thump-thumps his way up the steps, dragging his book bag. It's his second one this year—barely used. Mine is the same one I've had since sixth grade and it's on my back.

Whip and I have sat in different rows on the bus since the driver went nutso on us. Who would have thought shooting jellybeans from our noses would be that big a deal? But we figured out that if we wait for two more stops, the bus is packed enough that Whip can sneak into his old seat next to me, which he does today.

"Last night I was looking up Inca ruins on the computer," he says.

"Just last night?" I say. "You said it's due today, you moron."

"Whatever. Listen." He leans closer. "Dad was online before me and had turned off the parental controls. He forgot to turn them back on."

"So?"

"So, a pop-up ad came on. One of those asking if you're a good kisser. Not that I care about that, you know."

"No," I say. "Who would?"

"But I figured it might lead to something else, so I clicked it."

"Yeah?" I'm wondering why he's telling me this.

"I didn't find out how to kiss," he says, "but I found something *worth* kissing, if you know what I mean."

I don't.

He looks around, unzips the front pocket of his book bag, and pulls out a printout of a full-grown, honest-to-gosh buck-naked woman.

"Meet Jessica," he says.

When Whip shows me the picture, my mouth goes dry and my eyeballs hurt. He's looking at me and I know I have to say something but I don't know what, because:

Number one, I've never seen a naked girl before.

And number two, Whip looks happy! Whip, the guy who hates girls, is holding up a picture of this Jessica like he caught a prize fish.

Before I can think of an answer, the bus driver slams on the brakes. I get knocked forward into the back of the seat in front of me. The driver yells, "Stupid dog! You kids okay?"

Mom talks a lot about divine intervention. It's when something unexpected happens that changes your plans. For instance, if we decide to go to the movies but there's suddenly a plumbing problem and we have to wait for the super, Mom'll say, "It's divine intervention," meaning we weren't meant to go out that afternoon. I hate it when she says that.

When the bus stops moving, Whip shoves the picture back into his book bag. I gain a few extra seconds to let the hot feeling in my face cool off.

Divine intervention, definitely.

As soon as the driver sees we're all right, he hits the road again.

"So, what were we talking about?" I say to Whip, acting calm, as if seeing a naked girl for the first time is no big deal.

"Didn't you even see the picture?" he asks in a whisper that is louder than his regular voice.

"Oh, that. Yeah." I hope he doesn't ask what I think because I'm still not sure.

"So, what do you think?"

Man.

I mentally run through what I call my Oprah Archives. Mom watches *The Oprah Winfrey Show* every day. It's filmed here in Chicago and a friend took her to see it once. Now she's an Oprah fanatic. I don't get it, but I've found if I listen in I can mentally file away some good stuff to use on Mom later. Like the time I got out of going to Boy Scout meetings by telling her they were "crushing my spirit."

"How did it make *you* feel?" I say, turning the question around to Whip. It's one of Oprah's better ones.

The bus pulls up in front of school. He grabs his bag handle and stands up. "How'd you think I felt, freak?"

It works better when Oprah says it.

But now I know exactly why Mom doesn't want me on the Internet.

2

It takes until second period for my heart to stop knocking against my chest, pumping blood so hard I hear it roaring past my eardrums.

During gym class I concentrate on the basketball and the net. Ball. Net. Ball. Net. Skin. No!

I try to push the picture of "Jessica" out of my mind. Jessica. Cool name. No! Ball. Net. Ball. Net.

It isn't working.

In fourth-period art class, I sit leaning over my still-life charcoal sketch of fruit. I study the bowl with apples, grapes, and a tangerine. Then I notice the girl sitting next to it as she stretches and arches her back. I see the twin bumps under her shirt. I cough like a maniac to account for my red face.

"You okay?" the kid next to me asks.

I clear my throat. "Yeah." I get back to my drawing, too embarrassed to look again.

"There's only one tangerine." His voice pierces my thoughts.

"Huh?" I raise my head. He points to my picture with his piece of charcoal.

"We're supposed to draw the fruit that's on the table, not improvise."

I'm surprised to see I've drawn two tangerines, all right. Side by side, looking just like . . .

I could murder Whip. Only last year we made a pact never to date girls. Not even when we're old, like, thirty. We said girls were gross. The grossest of the gross. Spending time with them was worse than eating brussels sprouts, we said. Now he had to go and ruin it all with a picture that should make me gag instead of wanting to sneak another peek at a girl's shirt like a pervert.

I wad up my paper and start over.

"It wasn't that bad," the kid in my class says.

I want to say "Those weren't tangerines, either," but don't.

By the time school lets out, I've worked up a temper. I decide to tell Whip what he can do with his picture because I never want to see it again. I sit on the bus, waiting for him to slip back to my seat. He doesn't. I crane my neck, but he's busy talking to Rodney, the guy sitting next to him.

At our stop, I get off first. Whip follows.

"Shoot some hoops?" he asks, as if it's an ordinary day.

"Nah," I say, nonchalant, trying to match his mood. "Hey, about that picture you showed me today."

"Of Jessica," he says.

"Right."

"Jessica, Jessica." He sighs. "I'm gonna miss her."

"Miss her?"

"Yeah," he says. "She was something, all right. But you know whose picture is better than hers?"

My mouth goes dry again. How many naked girls is he going to pull out of his book bag?

"No," I squeak.

"Ben Franklin." He waves a five-dollar bill at me. "Rodney bought her."

"Oh." I shift my book bag. Divine intervention. I'll never get mad again when Mom says it because now my problem's solved. I won't have to feel like a perv for looking at something I shouldn't.

"What were you gonna say about her?" he asks.

I have no clue what to say now. "That her face looked familiar."

"Her *face*?" Whip says. "Who looked at her *face*? Are you sure you don't want to shoot some baskets?"

"Nah," I say. It's weird, but ever since Whip said he sold the picture, I feel like I was walking on a smooth road and tripped. "I think I'll get a snack."

For some reason I'm in the mood for fruit.

There isn't even a grape in the house. I finally find one lone granola bar behind the can of prunes Mom bought by mistake. I tear the wrapper from the bar and go straight into my bedroom. It's my job to keep my bed made. Since I get home before Mom, I always wait until after school, smoothing the covers over the bed, then doing a karate chop under the pillows.

I drop a scoop of cat food into Princess's dish, grab the glasses we used at bedtime and put them in the sink. The apartment is small, so we try to keep it neat. I know Mom was tired last night or she would have washed the glasses.

I check the menu on the refrigerator door. Tonight is macaroni and cheese, franks, and green beans. I open a can of beans, then dump them into a bowl and place them in the microwave. Next I fill two pans with water and set them on the stove, which is about all I can do until Mom gets home.

I turn around and see the computer staring at me. I think about Jessica. She's there somewhere, hiding inside that little black screen. The thought makes my ears feel hot.

I quickly turn back to the kitchen, squirt dishwashing soap into the sink, and scrub the glasses until they're so clean they make squeaky sounds when I run my finger down the sides. Then I look around and know that I'm out of jobs.

I let the soapy water drain away and dry my hands on my pants. I pour some juice into a cup, then walk over to the computer, pick up the Rubik's Cube, and set the juice in its place. The cube's always been the thing I turn to when I'm mad or trying to figure something out. It's made up of a lot of smaller cubes of six different colors that you twist and turn. If you're lucky, or very smart, you end up with one color only on each side of the larger cube. I've spent hours spinning it, thinking about my dad. Now as I flip it around, I wonder if Mom has parental controls on our computer. I get the yellow side almost done, take a swig of juice, and think, why would she? I mean there's no point if a parent is the only person who uses it.

I remember the day Uncle Peavey and Mom brought the computer home. "Wait until you see our surprise!" she had said with so much excitement that I figured it must come loaded with games for me. In the next breath, she'd said, "Now, don't touch it unless I'm home." Telling a kid you have a big surprise and he can't touch it is probably considered child abuse somewhere.

Remembering how disappointed I felt that day makes me so mad that I pick up the juice with one hand and toss the Rubik's Cube back onto the desk with the other. When I do, it bumps the mouse. The monitor screen lights up. I jump back.

Juice sloshes out of my cup onto the mouse pad.

Mom never leaves the power on. She had to be really tired last night, but knowing that doesn't help me now. That juice might as well be a neon sign that says EDDIE TOUCHED THE COMPUTER.

I throw the cup into the sink, grab a towel, and start sopping up the spill. I wipe all the juice away, but the pad is like a sponge. I rinse the juice off it and wring it as tight as I can, but it's still wet. I look at the clock. Mom will be home any minute now. Not knowing what else to do, I panic and run outside.

Whip is out front, iPod earbuds in, concentrating on his free throws. No sign of Mom. Whip shoots and misses. I snag the ball before he knows I'm there. He breaks into an ear-to-ear grin, then pulls out his headphones and stuffs them into the pocket of his pants. "Thought you weren't comin'!"

"Somebody's got to show you how it's done." I hold him back with my left hand, dribbling with my right. When he lunges to my right, I grab the ball, pivot, and throw. Swoosh!

"Nuthin' but net." I push the ball with both hands and bounce-pass it to him.

He wipes his face on the edge of his T-shirt. "Not bad, Eddie. Just don't forget who taught you."

I roll my eyes, but it's true. Whip taught me how to shoot. Heck, he even taught me how to ride a bike. But then, as I said, he lives with his dad. Having a father is crucial to knowing guy stuff, as anyone who was ever forced to watch *The Oprah Winfrey Show* will tell you.

"Your timing stinks, though," he says. "It's Tuesday."

"So?"

"So, Tuesdays are when . . . Dad's girlfriend comes. I have to let her in and, you know, keep her company until he gets here."

"I thought she came on Wednesdays."

"That's a different one," he says.

"Wow," I say. "How many girlfriends does he have?"

"Uh, two. Now help me push the hoop up."

Whip and I live for basketball. It's all we talk about. At least it was until this morning.

Part of basketball's draw is that Mom won't let Whip in our apartment if she's not home, or me in his if his dad isn't there. During our school breaks, if Whip and I want to spend time together, it has to be outside.

"I'm thirsty," he says. "Your turn."

We take turns each day getting pop from our apartments.

"We're out of drinks," I lie, but then to make up for it I say, "I'll do the next two days."

He drops the ball on my head and runs inside. Still no sign of Mom. Whip comes back, bringing out two Code Reds. Mom always buys the generic stuff, but Whip is a true friend. He never complains.

We sit on the front stoop and I think. On the one hand, I'm worried about Mom finding the wet mouse pad. On the other, I'm curious about what else Whip saw on the computer. Worry, left hand. Naked girls, right hand. Worry loses.

"So, Whip, I was thinking about your computer. You know, the parental controls. Are they on every time you go online?"

"Duh, yeah," he says. "Unless my dad shuts them off."

"How do you know if they're on or not?"

He cranes his head and eyeballs me. "Is this some lame joke? You act like you've never gone online before."

"I have, you know, at school."

"Your mom still won't let you, huh?"

"Nah," I say. "She's still afraid I'll blow up Argentina if I touch a wrong button."

"Then you've got the world by the butt, dude," Whip says. "Try and download a site. If you can, she doesn't have it blocked."

Why didn't I think of that? I chug my Code Red, then

wipe my mouth with the back of my hand. It's a little shaky because I want to act cool, but I can't help myself.

"That Web site you were on, the one you thought would be about kissing and stuff, what was it?"

"Man, I can't remember which one it was. Just look some up on a search engine."

"You've been on more than one?" I ask. "Why didn't you say somethin'?"

"It's not like I get on *all* the time, you know. Just sometimes when Dad forgets. Plus I didn't know if you'd be interested." He passes the ball back and forth between his hands.

"Oh," I say. Still not sure if I should be. I look at Whip. Now he's smiling like he has the best secret in the world.

"But if you thought Jessica was something, you should have seen Cherish." Then he just sits there, not saying another word, even though he knows good and well I want to hear more.

I nudge him.

"What?" he asks, looking like he has no idea what I want.

"Don't make me punch you, Jared."

He tries to keep a straight face but then busts out laughing.

"Oh, man, Cherish was the first one I found. I freaked. I didn't even think to print her." He shakes his head. "She was probably my all-time favorite. Not that I'd turn down a date with Jessica."

I snort. "A date! A date with *you*?" I must have laughed too hard. Whip gets that look that means I went too far.

"I'm just *saying*. Jeez, Eddie."

21

Whip's face is red. I take another sip of my drink, but he is quiet. I nudge him again. "Come on, dude."

"The thing is, Dad usually remembers to turn on the parental controls," he says in a sulking tone. "It's not like at your house. I mean, if your mom doesn't have controls, you're golden."

"Yeah, well, speaking of Mom, she'll be home any minute." I say this because I don't like the direction this conversation is taking. "I'd better go."

But Whip is getting into it. Before I can move, he puts his hands on my shoulders. "Why didn't we think of this before? Tomorrow, after school, we go straight to your apartment and get on your computer! It's perfect!"

He knows Mom doesn't allow him in our house when she's not there. I open my mouth to tell him no.

"You really are a genius!" he says.

But it wasn't my idea.

"No wonder you're in the advanced classes, man."

It was his idea and a bad one, but before I can say so, he shouts, *You are The Professor!*

And my traitorous mouth, when it should have been screaming no, splits into a grin that stretches totally across my face.

It's funny how when someone thinks you're smart, you feel smarter.

"I've got to go. I just thought of something," I say to Whip. "Catch ya later." Because I did think of something—how to save myself from Mom.

I barrel into our apartment and pick up the damp mouse

22

pad. I grab the blow dryer from the bathroom and turn that bad boy on high. The pad dries just in time.

I hear Mom call from the door. "Eddie! A little help here?"

She's struggling in the hall with her fold-up cart full of groceries and her book bag. The woman Whip was waiting for, one of Mr. Sweeney's girlfriends, walks by and asks Mom, "Do you need some help?"

"No, thank you." Mom's voice is sub-zero cold. She shouts, "Eddie!"

"Coming!" I call out, slipping the pad under the mouse as she turns her back. I grab the cart from her and begin unloading the sacks.

"I forgot you were getting groceries. I've been outside shooting with Wh—" I catch myself. She hates his nickname. "With Jared. I did the dishes. No homework tonight. How was your day?"

I'm babbling but can't stop myself.

"My day was brutal." She kicks off her shoes.

"Sit down. Got this under control," I say, and I have. Bread in the cupboard, canned goods down low. Perishables in the fridge.

I lay the Kraft mac and cheese box on its side, bringing a wooden spoon handle down hard onto the perforation. "Hiyah!" I peel back the top and pour the macaroni into one pan of water. I take four franks out of a package and pop them into the other pan, then push the button to nuke the beans.

"I could make this meal with my eyes closed," I say.

"You're probably right, but please don't." Mom takes her

long hair down and lays her head back on the couch. "I can see it now, hot dogs in the toaster, cheese packet sprinkled on the geranium, macaroni everywhere."

"That would be when *you* cook." I pop open a cola and hand it to her. She smiles her thanks and playfully swats me as I walk away. I rewind the tape that's in the VCR and turn on today's *Oprah* show for her.

"You're good to have around, Eddie McCall." She sighs, putting her feet up on the couch. "I couldn't ask for a better son."

And since I *haven't* used the computer, and I *haven't* let Whip into the apartment without Mom, I soak up the praise the way the mouse pad soaked up the juice.

3

Nothing I say the next day on the bus ride to school or back convinces Whip that it is not a good idea to use my mom's computer. We get off the bus and stand outside my apartment door.

"I really don't have that much time before Mom gets home."

"How much time?" Whip asks.

"I don't know. Just enough to shoot a few hoops with you, make my bed, start dinner. Maybe an hour."

"A whole hour?" His face lights up.

"Or maybe less, lots less, really. I just never know when she'll show up."

"Eddie, you worry too much," he says.

It occurs to me that I don't usually have a reason to worry unless Whip is involved.

Before I can say another word, he grabs the key out of my hand and jams it into the door lock. Never has our front door swinging open seemed so sinister. I expect to hear spooky music.

"Whip, I have to make my bed, straighten things, stuff like that. It really eats up the time," I try again, but he doesn't listen. He's already moved into Mom's desk chair.

"So, go," he says. "I'll surf till I find a good site."

I should go, but dread and curiosity root me to the spot.

He pushes the power button. The screen comes on, and after a minute he starts tapping out letters. Each peck at the keyboard gives me a pang of guilt. Standing at the scene of the crime doesn't feel too good, so I move to my bedroom. I take my time making my bed, the way I should every day. My hands are slow but everything inside—my brain, my pulse, my breath—is running a marathon. I look at the clock and want Whip to hurry and find a good site so he'll leave. But, just as much, I want him to find a good site and stay.

I smooth and tuck the bed until it's so tight you could bounce a quarter off it. I move on to the kitchen. Mom has done all the dishes. I feel Princess slinking around my ankles. I pick her up, intending to feed her, then look over and see what Whip has on the screen.

"Yeow!" I yell as Princess scratches me. I must have squeezed her. I let go and she jumps to the floor, giving me a betrayed look.

Now my hands move faster than lightning, throwing open the cabinet, scooping out a cup of cat food, and dumping it into her dish. Then I hurry over to Whip.

"What do ya think, Professor?" he asks.

I look at the screen and this time I don't have to wonder what to say. "She's beautiful."

"She's hot!" he says, hitting the print icon. "Her name is Delilah, but she's too old for us."

"Too old?" My voice sounds high to my ears. "It's not like we're gonna meet her."

"No, not her. But look what else I found." The screen minimizes and another screen is behind it. That one says *MatchesforTeens* at the top. In the corner there is a picture of a girl who would put even Jessica to shame. Her user name is Stormy, she's sixteen years old, and she lives in the Chicago area, just like us. She's not naked, just, well, *awesome*.

Despite my worry about Mom, I sit down on the couch behind Whip. Glide down is more like it.

"This is a dating service for teenagers," Whip says. "Can you believe it? We can actually *date* these girls!"

"Dating service," I whisper in awe.

"It's like ordering fast food, Eddie, only you end up with a hot date instead of cold pizza." His voice lowers to match mine. "We just sign up."

"We just sign up," I repeat.

"Snap out of it!" He punches me in the arm. "We need an e-mail account to join. I've already got one. What do you want your user name to be?"

I tear my eyes from the screen, but it's hard. Stormy's got this white blond hair sort of thrown over one raised shoulder, and her head tilts to one side. She's prettier than any girl at Randolph Middle School, and that includes the cheerleaders.

But I do stop looking at her and, when I do, the blood rushes back into my head. "Whip, I can't get e-mail! Mom'll know!"

"Not if we get you an account at free_email.com, you idiot. You have to sign in with a password and everything. She'll never know. Besides, the free_email program is already on this computer so it will be easy to set up an account." He pulls up a free_email register screen. "My user name is hoopmaster. Basketball, get it? What name do you want?"

I can't think, let alone talk.

"How about The Professor?" he says. When I don't answer, he types. "Man, I can't believe it's available. I had to try five to get mine," he says. "Okay, done. And your password?"

My brain hasn't worked since I saw Delilah.

"Geez, Eddie," he says, looking around. "How about Princess? Think you can remember your cat's name?"

It hits me that this is really happening. It's too cool. "Princess. That's a good one."

"Now I'll register you on the site." His fingers zip, filling in my info.

"Hey, I'm thirteen years old," I say, "not sixteen!"

He shakes his head, but his fingers don't miss a beat. "Minor detail. Once she meets you, it won't matter. And, uh, isn't it your turn for the soda?"

Meets me?

"Oh, yeah! Comin' right up!" She could meet me. I could meet her. I put one hand on the sofa arm and pivot-jump over Princess, so happy I feel I could fly. I pop the cans and decide, what the heck, I'll use glasses because this is an important occasion. The ice in the freezer is clumped together, so I take the handle of a spatula and chip at it, thinking, *theprofessor@free_email.com*. Having my very own e-mail address is almost as cool as a date with Stormy. Almost like I've become a man.

I set our drinks on the end table, then sit back beside Whip. That's when I hear Mom's key in the lock. Just a minute ago, everything looked bright, but that key rattle sucks all the color from my life. Now I know that I'm not The Professor or even Eddie McCall.

What I am is busted.

In the time it takes Mom to unlock the front door, Whip has closed out of the site, grabbed Delilah's picture, and shoved it under his shirt. He throws himself over the back of the sofa and is sitting there with an angelic look on his face. The only thing I've managed to do is pick up our drinks.

Mom takes in the scene, eyes squinting.

Whip calls out, "Hey, Ms. McCall! Nice to see ya!"

She transfers her lethal stare from Whip to me. Spies would crack under that stare.

"Thanks for the pop, Eddie," Whip says. I suddenly realize I'm holding the glasses and hand him one. It's hard to tell if it's condensation running down the glass or my sweat.

"Jared, I'm very *surprised* to see you here," Mom says, but she's looking at me.

"I forgot my key," he says. "Eddie felt sorry for me and said I could stay here until my, uh, my dad's girlfriend comes."

Whip is a master liar.

"Well, surely by the time you finish your drink *one* of your dad's girlfriends will be there," she says.

I wince. She could at least try to like him. But Whip doesn't seem to notice. He gulps down the soda and carries his glass over to the sink. He tucks his shirt in his waistband before turning around, and I remember that Delilah is under his shirt.

Mom has moved to the kitchen counter and is setting down her bag.

"I'll walk Whip home. Be right back!" I call, and quickly close the door before she sees something that tells her we were online.

I close the door and lean against it, shaking, but Whip raises his hand to high-five me. I lift a wimpy paw and he hits it so hard I'm surprised my hand isn't rolling down the hall, a lopsided bowling ball.

"We did it, dude!" he says.

"We almost got caught."

"There's no 'almost' to getting caught. You either do or you don't," he says. "Tomorrow we'll check our e-mail."

I spend the evening lying to my mom. "But Jared was locked out. What was I supposed to do?" I give her my very best innocent look while she grills me. After endless questions, she finally says, "Okay, you let him in, but just this once. Next time you can keep him company in the hall. He didn't have to wait *that* long."

Once the questions are over, Mom goes to the computer,

bumps the mouse, and the screen lights up. "I could have sworn I shut this off."

I about freak. "You were so tired last night you probably left it on," I say, sweat pouring off me.

"That's no excuse," she says. I know she means it was no excuse for her to leave it on but I want to say, "Best one I can come up with, spur of the moment."

Then Mom settles down to work and I'm free to think my thoughts. Mostly I think that I could actually end up on a date with someone like Stormy. A week ago I didn't even know I wanted a date. I still don't know what to do on one. There's no guy here to ask, and it's not like Whip would know. For a minute I think about Mr. Sweeney. He dates lots of girls. They may not be pretty, but now two come to his apartment every week—which gets Mom mumbling "commitment issues" under her breath. Besides, Mr. Sweeney's always so busy, and not just with dating. He seems to have a hard time working plus taking care of Jared and their apartment. As hard as it is for Mom to raise a kid alone, I think it's harder for Mr. Sweeney.

I go to bed at ten o'clock and, for the first time since I can remember, fall right to sleep. Until eleven-thirty, that is, when Mom bursts into my bedroom, flips on the light, and says, "Edward McCall, get your butt out here!"

I jump so high you'd think the bed ejected me. "What?"

"Now!" she growls. I get up and stumble, blinking, into the bright light of the living room.

"I knew I couldn't trust Jared in this house. I knew that

boy was up to no good. What can you expect from a kid whose father spends his time with bimbos instead of watching his child."

I've been through her rants before. Sometimes it's best to wait until Mom runs out of steam. It would have been easier on me, though, if she didn't have the *MatchesforTeens* site open on her computer.

"Oh, that boy looks innocent enough, but looks can be deceiving. And speaking of deceiving, you *lied* to me, Eddie!" She puts one hand on her hip. "You sat right there and lied to me."

At this point she's panting, so I wait a second. But then she says, "Don't you have anything to say?"

Then I know it's my turn. "Well, yeah, I do." My voice is so shaky that I sound guilty to my own ears.

Now both hands are on her hips. Not a good sign. "Well?"

"I shouldn't have got on the computer when you weren't home."

"You didn't just *get on the computer*! You signed up for this!" She points to the *MatchesforTeens* site.

"Well, yes, we did check out that site."

"And let's not forget your porn site!"

She's talking about Delilah! I wonder if it's possible to have a heart attack at the age of thirteen. I feel awfully close.

"I checked the Internet history, Eddie, so don't deny it."

"Okay," I try to say, but don't hear anything come out.

"And what other big rule did you break?" She is breathing hard, looking down at me like I'm a dog that just peed on her shoe.

"I let Whip into the house," I whisper.

"Call him Jared," she says. "You know how I hate that nickname."

Then something happens to me. I go from being meek Eddie, all apologetic, to being really mad Eddie because of the stupid rules that no other kid my age has to follow.

"Well, he wants to be called Whip, so that's his name. Maybe he doesn't like you being called Mom. Does that mean I should call you Linda?"

I see the storm gathering on her face, but I can't stop myself. "And I'd follow your rules except they're so lame! Any other mom would let a nice guy like Whip into her apartment. What'd he ever do to you?"

I point to the computer. "And that! Even three-year-olds play *Sesame Street* games online! I'm the only kid out of diapers who isn't allowed to use the freakin' Internet!"

I don't know if it's what I said, the way I said it, or that I used the word *freakin'*—which broke another rule—but the storm that was gathering on Mom's face explodes and I find myself in the middle of a category-five hurricane.

4

When Mom finally lets me go to bed—sentences me to bed is more like it—the clock says 1:13 a.m. I fall on top of the covers, facedown. I've seen pictures of torture victims in this same position, only they were held down by stakes. I'm weighed down by guilt.

Mom has me cold. From what I could pick up during her tirade, she was on the computer and an e-mail notice popped up from Stormy.

A little investigating from Mom, and life as I've known it is over. She takes everything away from me except air, and that's on loan. She says she's locking the computer mouse and keyboard in the closet every day so I can't go online again.

She could teach Bill Gates something about parental controls.

Mom says she is skipping her class tomorrow so she'll be home when I get out of school. And worst of all, I'm to have no contact with Whip. She says she'll "figure something out" about what to do with me this school break.

But the one thing I know is she can't miss work, so I'll see Whip on the bus in the morning. I finally fall asleep, only to be jarred awake by the alarm clock. My head has brain bruise from lack of sleep. I stagger into the bathroom and notice Mom forgot her usual note. Maybe she doesn't care enough anymore to remind me to brush my teeth. I splash water on my face wondering how I can make it through school as tired as I am. I think about skipping but I'm in enough trouble. I get dressed and walk into the living room, and there's my mom.

"What're you doing here?" I croak with early morning voice.

"Well, it's not like I want to miss work," she says. "But it appears I don't have any support in this mess from Samuel Sweeney with his 'boys will be boys' attitude. He's doing nothing to keep you two apart."

She crosses her legs, and her foot swings up and down. I've always been able to tell how mad she is by how high her foot bounces. If it were measured by the Richter scale, it would be a ten.

"Since I can't trust you with Jared, I don't have much choice but to take you to school myself."

"What do you think's gonna happen on the bus? That Whip will bring a laptop and together we'll hack into Microsoft?" I mumble this so she can't hear all of it as I hold my aching head in my hands. Then I raise my head and my voice. "And you called Mr. Sweeney? You got Whip into trouble?"

"Who?" Her eyes narrow.

I say as defiantly as I can, "Whip," feeling like Harry Potter using He-Who-Must-Not-Be-Named's name.

"*Jared* got himself into trouble," Mom says. "Except that he's not in trouble because his father doesn't agree. He actually told me to 'chill and stop sweating the small stuff'!"

Wow! Mr. Sweeney shoots, he scores!

I look down quickly, so far down my chin almost touches my chest, because I don't want her to see my happy expression. Mr. Sweeney is my new hero.

She jumps up, goes into the kitchen, and brings back a plate with scrambled eggs and toast, plus a glass of milk. The only good thing about having her home.

"Thanks," I mumble, then gulp the milk and tear into breakfast.

Mom paces in front of me as I eat, pulling her hair into a ponytail. "Since it's obvious I can't trust you at home this summer, I called Uncle Peavey last night." She stops and looks at me. "He will be driving here to pick you up. You'll be spending your school break in Indiana with him."

"What?" I spew yellow egg gunk across the room.

"Eddie, look what you did!"

"Well, jeez, what'd you expect? I've never even been there!"

Her mouth goes into a tight line. "We haven't gone because there's nothing there for me except Uncle Peavey, and he visits us here. There's no reason for me to go back."

"You think there's something there for me?" I can't believe this. "You're sending me into the land of soy beans with an old guy I barely know! And all over what, Mom? Sure, I broke your rules. I'm sorry you're mad but—" I hesitate, knowing this is where I should stop, but Mr. Sweeney's words are still rattling around in my head. "Your rules aren't even realistic. Maybe the problem isn't me. Maybe you just need to lighten up."

"That does it, young man! That. Does. It!" She rips the plate out of my hands. "Forget about school today and tomorrow. You're finished with finals, anyway. You'll be on your way to Uncle Peavey's as soon as I can arrange it. And I'm spending the day with you."

Normally I'd be thrilled to skip school. But I don't know Uncle Peavey very well, and, to be honest, he's not someone I want to know. He's got gross-out fingernails caked with grease that scared me when I was a kid. Mom used to tell me it's because he's a hard worker, but no one I know has black claws like that. The guy comes with a can that he spits tobacco juice in, for heaven's sake.

And I'm glad Whip's not in trouble with his dad. Really I am. But this is so typical of our lives. Whip started all this. He got on Mom's computer and signed us up. He did it all and he's not in trouble, but I'm spending four weeks with a complete stranger.

I'd cut my tongue out before telling Mom, but right now I don't think I like Whip much more than she does.

Mom has to borrow a suitcase from her friend, since we never go anywhere and don't own one. She loads my backpack with granola bars ("In case you get hungry"), a phone card ("So you can call home"), and two twenty-dollar bills ("So you won't have to ask Uncle Peavey for anything"). I feel so much resentment bubbling up I could choke on it when I think of the kids at school who pull wadded bills out of their pockets like used gum wrappers and feed them into vending machines while I have to eat the reduced-price hot lunch. I think of Whip and the other guys there, walking around with cell phones stuck to their ears. I want to tell her to keep her snacks, her calling card, and her measly forty bucks. Then I feel guilty because I know what she's given me is all she's got.

The next morning it's early, so early the sun isn't up, as we ride the train to Michigan Avenue, to Mom's job. She tries to make small talk but gives up when all she gets from me are grunts. We reach the Hilltop at 5:20 a.m.

Mom says, "You can hang out upstairs." They have a cafeteria for the employees on the fourteenth floor.

"Whatever." I don't even look at her.

Her eyes land on the gift shop. "Don't buy that over-priced food. Eat what's in your backpack."

"Yeah, I'll miss you, too."

"Oh, Eddie." Her eyes fill with tears, making me wish I'd kept my mouth shut. "I don't want it to be like this! What will I do without you for a month?"

"You should have thought about that before you decided to ship me off. This guy is practically a stranger, Mom."

"What a thing to say! Uncle Peavey is your grandfather's brother, for heaven's sake."

"We've hardly spent any time with him." I pick at a scab

on my hand. "For all we know, he could be a child molester."
Doesn't she read the missing-children literature the school
sends home?

"Oh, good grief!" she says. "Eddie, he's my uncle. He's a
very nice man. You have nothing to worry about."

She reaches for me. I step back and see the hurt in her
eyes, but right now I don't care. She's wrong. That's all I
know.

Mom lets out a big sigh and hurries off to set out the pas-
tries and fruit before the crowd hits.

I'm so mad I walk straight to the gift shop and buy a root
beer and a bag of Cheezems from a girl in a tight pink
T-shirt. I remember Whip saying, "Her *face*? Who looked at
her *face*?" and wonder if I'll ever again notice anything about
a girl except what's in her shirt.

I sit down to eat. Normally I'd be happy to be here. The
hotel reminds me of a palace. Movie stars and presidents have
stayed here, but the best part is that it's a place where movies
were filmed. I think Mom's got the best job in the world,
working in such a cool place, but she's taking classes to get a
business degree. She says, "I like my job, but I've set my
sights higher."

Not me. When I grow up I want to be one of the con-
cierges here. People line up just to ask them questions. But I
don't tell Mom this. She's set her sights higher for me, too.

I kill a few hours pretending I'm one of the guests, until
it's time for Whip to arrive at school. I'm no longer mad at
him and I know that if I don't tell him where I'm going,
Mom never will.

I go downstairs and sit at one of the pay phones, pull out the calling card, and dial Whip's cell number.

"You got Sweeney." He answers it differently every time.

"Whip?" I say.

"Eddie! I wanted to call you after school yesterday, but my dad wouldn't let me. Are you sick or somethin'?"

"Nah, Stormy e-mailed me when Mom was on the computer. Mom is madder than I've ever seen her. She pulled me outa school and is sending me out of town for a month."

"Sa-weet!" he says. "Stormy e-mailed you? Awesome, dude!"

Until that minute I didn't really think much about the fact that it *was* awesome. Then I remember it's a moot point, to use last week's vocab word.

"Whip, listen to me. I'm leaving for Indiana to stay with my mom's uncle. I won't be at school today either, and I won't see you all vacation break."

"That bites," Whip says. "But isn't he the old guy who's loaded? The one who sends you gifts and stuff?"

Sometimes getting Whip to focus is like having a staring contest with a mad wasp.

"You're not hearing the important part. Mom doesn't want me to have anything to do with you. She thinks you're a bad influence."

"That'll wear off. You know parents. They get tired of being mad."

He obviously doesn't know my mom.

"Besides," he says, "you're always talking about how you

wish you had a dad. Maybe this uncle will be kind of a stand-in. He's probably so rich he'll pick you up in a Cadillac."

I think of Uncle Peavey's plain clothes when he visits and can't imagine he's rolling in money, but I hate to say that to Whip. I get so tired of Mom and me being broke when Whip has so much.

"Has he got a bunch of kids?" he asks.

"No, just me and my mom."

"See? You hit the jackpot, Eddie. I am so jealous. He's probably got a huge house with a swimming pool. You won't even want to come back."

Whip has a way of looking at things that I never would. I mean, I guess it's possible Uncle Peavey's got money. He does give nice gifts. Before I can even think about what he's say-ing, he adds, "When you get there, check your e-mail ac-count. Maybe Stormy's not the only girl to contact you. I'll have to live through you. Your mom came before I signed myself up."

"Oh. Sorry."

"It's okay. Gonna be late for class, man. It'll be a long break without you. Call when you can. Or, hey, have his maid call!" I hear him laughing as he clicks off.

I slowly hang up the phone and realize that I probably won't be able to use Uncle Peavey's computer to check my e-mail because Mom will tell him what happened. Mom may be the only person in the universe who overreacts to using the Internet, but it will be really embarrassing if he knows about the porn thing.

When I come upstairs, Mom is talking to a short, skinny bald guy with big black glasses—Uncle Peavey. I have a sinking feeling at the place where my Cheezems are now resting, and even though I'm a teenager, I want to cry because it's really happening. My mom is sending me away for the first time.

$\boxed{5}$

This way, Ed." He gestures to the right, then pulls out a cap and puts it on his head. It says SEED CORN on it. Perfect.

I look at the truck he's pointing out. Definitely not the Cadillac Whip predicted. Maybe he meant another vehicle.

"Are you talking about the white truck, Uncle Peavey?"

He walks toward the truck and says, "Yep. Just Peavey'll do, though. I don't expect to call you Nephew Ed."

He climbs in, starts the truck, and sits there. I don't want to get in, but my options are limited, so I toss my suitcase and backpack into the bed of his truck. I open the door and hesitate, realizing that I may be setting myself up for a lecture on the misuse of computers.

He turns to me and says, "Ed, you might want to close the door while you're thinking." He nods toward the truck's air conditioner. "You can take all the time you need, but right now you're letting out the bought air."

"Oh!" I say, and quickly climb in.

"Somethin' on your mind?" he asks.

"Well, yeah, Unc—I mean, Peavey." His name hangs so heavy in the air I feel as if I could touch it. "I guess I'm wondering why Mom asked you to take me for break."

"She didn't want you left at home during the day. Wanted you to stay busy. Not have time to run around with a friend she doesn't approve of."

No mention of the Internet. I feel better already.

"Anything else I should know about?" Peavey asks.

"Nope. That's it," I say. I mean, if Mom doesn't think he needs to know about the Internet, why should I tell him?

After riding for almost two hours, we pass a Burger King, and I don't know if it's because it's one thing in this strange place that looks familiar to me or if my snack has worn off, but I want to stop. Peavey doesn't offer, so I keep my mouth shut. A half hour later, though, the root beer I had earlier has got to come out.

He hasn't said one word since we started, so I ask, "Is it still far to your house?"

"Not too" is all he says.

In another ten minutes, I say, "I really need to find a restroom."

"Easy enough." He flips on his turn signal and pulls off onto a gravel road.

"Are we having car trouble?" I ask.

"Nah, there's a big tree if you've got to go."

I laugh. "You're kidding, right?"

One look at him and I know he's not.

"You said you had to go."

"Well, yeah, but I can wait until we find a McDonald's."

He doesn't answer, just pulls back onto the highway until we come to a gas station. I can't get out of the truck fast enough, both for my bulging bladder and just to get away from him for a few. I'm starting to wonder if Peavey's all there. I decide that tonight I'll sleep with a night-light.

We drive on until he pulls into a town called Sheldon. We get to the end of about the sixth block and there is a Kelley's Konvenience Store, just like the ones in Chicago, only this one has just two gas pumps out front. Sort of a mini Kelley's. Next to it stands a small old white house with an enormous barn behind it. Past the house is a new-looking house, and beyond that, a couple more are just being built. I think Peavey's is the new one, but he pulls into the driveway by the old house and shuts off the truck.

I sit there. "This is it?"

"Yep," he says.

The house has a porch that goes across the front. There is a roof on the porch with little spindles all over it, making the porch look like a birthday cake with a row of candles on top. At the peak of the house is a wooden piece with all kinds of curlicues carved into it. The whole thing is tiny, needs paint, and looks ancient. I didn't buy Whip's theory that Peavey was rich, exactly, but he always gave us nice gifts so I did kind of think he'd have a better place.

Peavey is standing next to the truck, rolling his hat in his hands. I shrug off my disappointment as best I can, grab my

45

bags, and follow as he steps inside the house, holding the door open for me. I walk into a small room with only a chair, a recliner, and a television set.

"Before I show you around, I promised Boo you'd call and tell her you arrived safe."

"Who is Boo?"

"Your mom, Lindy. That kid'd play peek-a-boo with a mirror if she ran out of people." He smiles for the first time and shows an alarming amount of upper gum. "Guess no one but me calls her that now. Old habits die hard. Well, you give her a call. I promised."

I didn't even know my mom was called Lindy, let alone Boo. And after the way she acted about Whip's nickname! I'm so mad I fumble and drop the calling card.

"And don't be usin' that thing. I told her I could spot a few phone calls."

I don't know what *spot* means and I'm too mad to ask. No way can I talk to my mom, *Boo*, right now. I wish I could let her know I'm here without talking to her. E-mail would be great. Then it hits me that if Peavey doesn't know about my getting busted on the Internet, he might let me use his. I wouldn't actually e-mail Mom, but I could use that as an excuse to go online. Maybe Stormy e-mailed me. Or, like Whip said, some other girl from *Matchesfor Teens*.

"Um, I don't think she's home right now. How about I just e-mail her?"

"Can't."

My heart sinks. He must know more than he's letting on. I look at my fingernails so he won't see my red face.

"Don't own a computer."

"You don't?" I find that incredible. "But everyone owns a computer. You even bought us one!"

He nods. "When Boo decided to go back to school, I figured she'd need one. I've got no use for one, though. Now call your mom."

I force myself to walk toward the phone. Peavey says, "The library's just a few blocks away, though. They have computers and Internet and such. I'll take you there soon and get you set up so you can e-mail."

My mood picks up considerably at that. It never occurred to me to go to the library to use a computer. Just thinking about being able to get on the Internet whenever I want could make the stay here worthwhile.

I can't make myself call Mom, but Whip takes early lunch at school and it's about that time, so I punch in his cell number.

"Miracle Whip here," he says.

"Hey, Whip, it's Eddie."

"Professor! Is the old dude rich?"

"Uh . . . we'll talk later. Listen, I need you to do me a favor. When Mom gets home tonight, tell her I made it here okay."

"Why don't you just call her yourself?"

"Long story."

"I don't know, Eddie. She doesn't like me. It's no secret."

I whisper, "I need this favor, man."

"Well, okay, but you have to give me details later. I'll e-mail and let you know how it goes with your mom."

I hang up and Peavey is standing about two feet from me. "I, uh, she's not home now, so I called a neighbor. He's reliable."

Peavey nods to show he understands. "This is the parlor. On past is the kitchen."

I follow him, and find the oldest table I've ever seen in the middle of the room. It has legs so spindly you'd think a full meal would make them buckle. When Peavey isn't looking I lean on the table, but it stands just fine. The chairs all have narrow, high backs. His kitchen cabinets are white metal, and his refrigerator isn't any taller than I am. I feel as though I've stepped into a time machine. Aunt Bea has newer stuff on the reruns of *The Andy Griffith Show*.

Peavey opens a door at the side of the kitchen. "Just off here is the folks' bedroom."

I get a quick look at a bed with a quilt on it before he shoves the door shut, waving a musty, unused smell toward me. He opens another door. "Commode and shower are in here."

"What's a commode?"

"Well, Ed, a commode is a toilet."

Why didn't you just say that? But I keep my lips pressed together. He climbs some narrow winding stairs. Upstairs there is just one bedroom with bunk beds.

"This here is my bed." He points to the bottom. "I had the top till your grandpa Emery got married."

"And you still sleep in here?" I say, hoping I don't sound rude.

"I'm not the one that got married and left. Where else would I sleep?"

"Well, don't you own the house now? I mean, aren't you the only one that lives here?"

"Till now," he says, reminding me that I have to sleep here tonight.

"I just would have thought you'd take the downstairs bedroom or maybe put a big bed in here, that's all."

"This bed's done right by me so far," he says. "You can take the top bunk. I don't snore, but then I don't have anyone to back me up on that. Or, if you've a mind, you can sleep in the folks' room. Your choice."

I act like I'm thinking real hard, but what I'm really thinking is that I can't stay in this creepy house. "Can I let you know?"

He nods. Then we hear a voice downstairs. "Yoo-hoo! Peavey? You here?"

"That would be Ordella Mae," he says.

Oh, God, I think. *Whoever she is, please let her be sane.*

I follow Peavey downstairs and see a woman struggling to carry a big pot through the door. I run over and grab one side of it, helping her set it on the stove.

"Well, aren't you a gentleman!" she says, pushing the curly gray hair off her forehead.

"This is Lindy's boy, Ed," Peavey says. "Ed, Ordella Mae."

She holds out her hand to shake mine. Normally when grownups shake your hand you can tell they think you're just a punk kid but want to make you feel grown up. Ordella Mae is different. She looks me right in the eye and really smiles, so I give her hand a shake.

"Most people call me Della," she says.

"Most people call me Eddie," I answer back.

She chuckles. "Well, Eddie, it's good to meet you. It's been a long time since I've seen your mom, but I would have known you were her son."

"You knew my mom?" I ask.

"Of course. She was the apple of this whole family's eye, wasn't she, Peavey?"

Peavey nods once.

"So are you and I . . . related?" I ask her.

"Not by blood." Ordella pulls out a cigarette from her purse and lights it. I've never seen an adult do that indoors before. The stats for dying from secondhand smoke flash through my brain as she inhales. "My late husband, Arthur, and your uncle, Peavey, were best friends." Smoke blows out her nose in spurts as she talks. "And of course your grandpa, Emery, was always around. Our kids, Arthur's and mine, were almost raised before your grandpa finally got married and had Linda, so we all spoiled her rotten."

She turns and flips her ashes into the kitchen sink.

"Ordella," Peavey says, frowning.

"Peavey, I would be more than happy to use an ashtray, but you don't have any." Her words are even, but the look on her face says they've had this discussion before.

"There's a reason for that, as you good and well know," he says.

"Now, don't go getting holier than thou about my smoking when you chew. Tobacco is tobacco, Peavey."

I clear my throat and change the subject because I'm afraid an argument is going to start. "Is there anything else you need brought in?"

"No. Glad you reminded me, though." She opens the pan lid, sticks the cigarette in her mouth, and talks at the same time. "These beef and noodles ought to last you boys for a few days." She reaches for a spoon and gives them a big stir, making me nervous that her ashes will fall into the pot.

She finally takes the cigarette out of her mouth. "I cook part-time at the Senior Citizens' Center. It's a nice place. We offer fellowship, games, food, but do you think I can talk Peavey into coming? My face would be a permanent shade of blue if I tried. No, I've given up, but I do bring him dinner a few times a week. We'd have to throw it out, anyway."

I'm not that thrilled to know I'll be eating food that was one step away from a trash can. Still, my stomach growls at the good smell coming from the pot.

"I need to be going or I'll be late for my game." Della sticks her cigarette back in her mouth and brushes away ashes. She isn't heavy, but she does have a good-sized ball of belly, which she smooths her T-shirt over. I notice that her shirt says BUNCO BABE.

"Come see me off," she says, so Peavey and I follow her outside. "I'm sure you and I will be seeing a lot of each other, Eddie." Then she tells me in a whisper loud enough for Peavey to hear, "He doesn't talk much, but he's okay."

She waves, climbs into her big old car, and guns it down

the road, sending exhaust fumes to mingle with the cigarette smoke. I look at Peavey. He puts his cap on his bald head. With his big, black glasses sticking out from his face, he reminds me of a garden gnome someone has dressed up.

Cigarettes, weird shirt, and all, Della is the one I'd rather be stuck with.

6

Peavey just stands there. So do I. No one's talking, but he begins whistling. I don't mean a song, just one long note, and he's staring somewhere above my head. I'm not used to adults who don't fill the air with words. I put my hands in my pockets to have something to do.

My stomach growls again, and he suddenly looks at his watch, then at me. "Noon or there 'bouts. We should eat." He goes into the kitchen and I follow. He opens one of the white cabinets, pulls out a lace cloth, and smooths it over the table.

"You're company. My mother always said it's important to put on a nice tablecloth for company."

I could take or leave the cloth, but it's nice he's making an effort for me. Next he gets out a plate and a tumbler that he fills with water. He scoops a few noodles from the pan Della left on the stove and rummages around in a drawer until he finds a fork. I hold out my hand, about to say thanks,

when he leans against the sink and begins shoveling the noodles into his mouth.

I quickly put my hand down, embarrassed and confused
about what to do next.

He doesn't look up, just mumbles with his mouth full.
"Get a plate, Ed. Help yourself."

A ball of jumbled-up feelings clog my throat. I don't see
how I'll be able to swallow past them, but I get out a plate,
tumbler, and fork to have something to do until the feelings
pass. I sit at the table. Still leaning against the sink, Peavey
never looks up.

I force a bite into my mouth. The food really is good and
I'm able to eat some. When Peavey's finished, he rinses his
utensils off in water, then puts them in a dish drainer. No
soap used. I stop eating mid-chew, wondering how many
germs I just ingested off the plate.

"I'll be in the barn. Come on out and meet Ronnie when
you're through," he says, still not looking at me.

I force myself to swallow. "Who's Ronnie?"

"Ronnie Fielding. Helps me in the mowin' business," he
says. I watch him walk, one leg a little stiffer than the other,
causing him to lean to the left with every other step.

When he disappears into the barn, I hurry to the sink, fill
it with dishwashing soap and water, and take not only the
dishes he just rinsed off but all the plates, glasses, and silverware in the cabinets and dump them in. I'll never be able to
eat here unless I know the stuff's clean. I'm wondering how
many granola bars Mom sent with me, because what with

Peavey's weird eating habits and unsanitary utensils, I imagine I'm going to be pretty hungry.

I quickly dry the dishes and silverware and put them back into the cabinets and drawers. I set the pan of noodles inside the refrigerator, then join Peavey in the barn.

He's wearing safety goggles and is sharpening blades on a grinder. The noise is loud and Peavey is lost in his job. I look around and see this Ronnie guy wearing coveralls and bent over a motor. He's got longish, almost black hair, and is even shorter than Peavey, which makes me wonder if there's something in Indiana water that causes stunted growth. Ronnie still hasn't noticed me and I'm not up to starting a conversation, so I head out the barn door. I see the Kelley's Konvenience Store sign and decide to walk over and check out what they have.

This Kelley's is smaller than the ones I've seen. There is just one cash register, but the store has the usual: candy, pop, snacks, milk, and a few boxed foods. There is also a window where you can order pizza and fountain pop. The way things are looking at Peavey's, I may be spending a lot of time here to keep starvation away. I squat at the canned pop display, eye level with the Mountain Dew, and try to get my willpower to kick in so I can save my money when a girl's voice asks, "May I help you?"

I look up from where I've squatted at the most amazing creature I've ever seen. I stand too fast and get a head rush, but I might have gotten it anyway, just from looking at her.

"I—" is all I get out. She smiles, and her teeth are almost

blinding white. She has dark hair with sort of purplish streaks through it. Her hair is long around her face but spiked short on top. She just looks *fine*.

"If you need anything, I'll be over here," she says.

I watch her walk away, the pockets on the back of her jeans doing a little dance as she goes. Fast, short breaths come out of me as I grab a pack of gum so I'll have a reason to follow her.

She picks the gum up from where I set it on the counter and scans it. I hand her a dollar. She's wearing a tight shirt that ends about an inch above her belt, and a small star dangles from her bare navel. I can't take my eyes off it, which isn't good because she hands back the change and I drop it. She laughs, so I do, too. Her laugh sounds genuine, like a tinkling bell. Mine sounds too loud and fake to my own ears. I gather up the money and head for the door.

"You forgot this."

I look back. She's holding out my pack of gum. I reach for it and feel her hand when I do. It's warm. So is my gum. I'll keep it forever. Well, I might chew the gum, but the package I'll keep.

My head is so light I think it will float off as I head back to Peavey's. She'd said, "If you need anything, I'll be over here." It's not something I'll forget.

I get back to the barn, and the boy, Ronnie, is standing with his hands on his hips, talking to Peavey. He sees me and shuts up. I half wave and he turns away. Peavey looks over his shoulder and, seeing me, swivels on his good leg so he's facing us both.

"There you are. Must be a big eater."

"Or just doesn't like to work," Ronnie mutters.

At first I'm confused, then realize they think I've been in the house all this time.

"I came out. You were busy, so I went to the store next door." I hold up my pack of gum as proof.

"Then you've met Erin," Peavey says.

"You mean that awesome-looking girl?" I ask.

Ronnie picks up a greasy machine part, wiping it roughly with a rag. Peavey looks down. "Well, she's pretty, I guess. She's Ronnie's sister."

"Oh, sorry, Ronnie." I figure he must be ticked, the way he's attacking that piece of metal. "I didn't mean anything by it. She was just nice and, well, really pretty."

He drops the motor part with a thud onto the bench. I say, "Hey, really, I'm sorry. I didn't mean any disrespect. I guess some guys get touchy if people talk about their sisters."

Ronnie's eyes burn into mine. "What did you say?"

I'm wondering if my interest in Erin is showing on my face. I can't figure out why he's so mad.

"I said—"

"I heard what you said!"

Peavey clears his throat. "Maybe I can clear this up, Ed. Ronnie here is Erin's sister. Her given name is Veronica."

It takes a minute for it to soak in. I look back and, yeah, I guess Ronnie could be a girl. Well, *is* a girl. She's got the same thick eyelashes, and her hair is as dark as the part of Erin's that's not purple. Of course, Erin wears makeup, and Ronnie obviously doesn't.

"I'm really sorry," I say. "But, you know, with a name like Ronnie . . . and you're wearing coveralls . . . How old are you?"

She just glares, so Peavey answers, "Ronnie's thirteen, same as you."

"Which is none of your business, Mr. Big City," she says. "Peavey, I'm pretty much done for the day."

"Oh," he says. "Well . . ."

"See you tomorrow," she says to him, then throws her greasy rag at me. I catch it without thinking, but drop my pack of gum. She sees it fall and steps on it as she walks out. Not just a light step, either, sort of a twist-grind step. I grab the gum and wipe it on my T-shirt, but it will never be the same.

"What's her problem?" I ask Peavey.

"Well, there's a little what they call 'sibling rivalry' between the girls. Erin gets a lot of attention because she's pretty and smart. Plus there's three years' age difference. Ronnie's young and folks can't always see what a crackerjack of a girl she is right off."

"It might help if she dressed like one."

"Doesn't matter what a person wears, Ed. Ronnie's got a good heart and is the best mechanic I've ever met."

"But most mechanics are guys. She dresses like a guy, then gets ticked off when I think she *is* one!"

Peavey hangs tools on a Peg-Board and says, "Next time you'll know to treat her like a girl."

His words really hit me because I *don't* know how to treat a girl. It's just Peavey and me in the barn, and I wish he were

58

the kind of guy you could ask about things like that. He nods toward a tool and I hand it to him. He grunts his thanks, which kills any desire I had to ask him anything. I sigh.

He looks up. "Something on your mind?"

I say the first thing that comes into my head. "I wish I knew my dad."

He begins that long, low one-note whistle again. I have no idea if that means I should shut up. I keep talking.

"My mom won't tell me about him." Then it hits me that Peavey might have known him.

"Did you ever meet him?"

He whistles louder.

"Mom won't even tell me his name."

He finally stops whistling but doesn't look at me. "If Lindy doesn't talk to you about your dad, she's got her reasons."

Silence on the subject, it would appear, runs in our family.

"Well, you can't talk to your mom about everything, you know," I say. "There are some things you just need to go to a guy about."

"Such as?"

"Well, let's just say I was old enough to date." I nearly choke on the words but force myself to finish. "Or get married. That's stuff you'd want a guy's opinion on, right?"

I hand him the last tool. He hangs it and wipes his hands on a rag. He looks above my head and I think to myself that if he does the weird whistle instead of answering me, I will walk back to Chicago.

"I've never been married, but I did come close once," he says.

Finally, we're getting somewhere. I pull a stool next to him, ready to absorb any guy knowledge he wants to part with.

When he doesn't say anything else, I ask, "What happened?"

"I never got up the courage to ask her—"

"Oh, that's too bad."

"—for a date."

After dinner—noodles again—I fill the sink and wash the dishes. Peavey looks a little surprised, but he'll have to get used to it.

We watch TV, or at least he does. I sit there fuming, wondering how I can be related to such a loser and, deep down, wondering if I'm a loser, too. I didn't realize how much I expected from him until now.

He's never even been on a date. Never even *asked* a girl for one. I scrunch down lower in the chair, pulling my head into my collar like a turtle.

Next thing I know, he nudges my shoulder.

"You fell asleep," he says. I look around, confused at first. Then I remember I'm stuck in a hick town with a loser.

I rub my eyes, trying to wake up. He says, "It's okay. You've had a long day. Have you made up your mind where you're sleepin' yet?"

Aw, jeez. It's back to that. No way am I sleeping in the same room as this guy.

"I guess I'll sleep down here."

He nods and opens his parents' bedroom door.

"Um, I was thinking of sleeping on the couch."

"Got no couch, Ed. Guess you were too tired to notice." He smiles a little, then looks away. He scratches his head. "Well, I guess I'll say good night now. Holler if you need anything."

He climbs the stairs to go to bed. I look around. There really isn't a place to sleep in the living room, although I consider the chair. I mean, I fell asleep there once, didn't I? But already my neck feels sore from the short time I spent there. I walk into the bedroom. My dead great-grandparents' room. Can this get any creepier? There are white ruffled curtains at the window with a blind pulled down. Old pictures line the dresser. I hold up one of two little boys, who must be Peavey and my grandpa. I barely remember him, but surely he wasn't weird like Peavey. I tell myself that Mom's not weird and feel a little calmer. Then I remember that she sent me here, and I'm not so sure.

I look at the bed and don't even want to touch it. I decide to sleep on the floor with clothes and shoes on. I use my backpack as a pillow and wish I had a blanket to pull over my head. This time I'd welcome the carbon dioxide.

7

I wake up hearing Peavey stir his coffee over and over again. The clanking sound pierces my skull. I slowly uncurl and sit up, every muscle in my body stiff. My stomach is so empty it's probably feeding on itself. I open the door, wondering if noodles are on the menu for breakfast, too.

I don't smell anything cooking when I step into the kitchen. Peavey has a piece of dry toast next to his coffee. At least he's sitting at the table. He looks up from his newspaper.

"Mornin'," he says. "Toaster's by the stove if you want breakfast."

I open his refrigerator for some milk and see only a can of condensed. My stomach tightens. I think I'll skip breakfast.

I hear a motor rumbling and see Della's car pull up. She gets out holding a plate of food. I perk up, excited about whatever it is. Happy to see her.

Peavey holds the door open for her. "Ordella Mae," he says.

Della stops on the top step and says, "Peavey, have you heard? I just got word that Arnetta Daly is very ill."

Peavey shakes his head. "Can't say I have."

He has a frown on his face and I wonder if this sick person is close to him, but he just says, "Ed's up bright and early this morning."

"Oh, good morning, Eddie! I didn't see you there."

"Hi." My voice cracks. I try again. "Is Arnetta Daly family, Peavey?"

"No one you need concern yourself with," he says.

"Don't mind us," Della says, coming into the kitchen with Peavey. "Old people in a small town have nothing better to do than spread the word when someone older is sick or dying. I made up a batch of monkey bread last night. Have you ever had monkey bread, Eddie?"

"No, I haven't."

It's shaped like a Bundt cake, but it's made of small balls of dough packed together with nuts and sticky-looking stuff all over it. I want to reach for a piece, but I see a scowl forming on her face.

"Aren't those the clothes you wore yesterday? Did you bring more?"

"I did," I say, looking down so she won't see that I'm embarrassed. "I just haven't changed yet."

"You slept in those." She states it, doesn't ask, so I don't answer. She sets the monkey bread on the table and puts one hand on her hip.

"Eddie, where did you sleep last night?"

I point to the bedroom. She heads toward it and, even

though the monkey bread smells delicious, I feel I should follow her.

"You made the bed already?" I hesitate and she looks at my backpack on the floor, still dented from my head. "Never mind. You slept on the floor, didn't you?"

She flies past me back to the kitchen. "Peavey, let's go outside."

Slamming the door, she heads for the yard and lights up a cigarette. Peavey sighs big-time. He heaves himself out of the chair and follows her. I can't hear what they're saying. She's gesturing and in his face. He stands there and takes it. I, on the other hand, pull off pieces of monkey bread and stuff the gooey, sugary goodness into my mouth.

I see Della climb into her car and pull away fast, like she's mad, which disappoints me. I feel better when she's around.

Peavey walks in and picks up the paper he's been reading. Without a word to me, he begins laying the sheets of newspaper on the floor. At first I'm kind of fascinated. Then I realize this isn't normal behavior, but I have dough balled in my mouth so tight it's stuck to the roof of my mouth.

I get a glass of water and wash the bread down.

"What are you doing?"

"Well, Ed, yesterday you were company. Today you live here, same as me."

He says this as if it answers my question. He takes the tablecloth, folds it, and sticks it back in the drawer. I wonder if this guy ever washes anything. Next he goes into the laundry room and brings back a stack of old newspapers, continuing to lay them down throughout the house.

I ask, "But what's the newspaper for?"

"Mud. Dirt." Then his head does a kind of Egyptian head-sliding thing and he says, "Because despite what Ordella thinks, this *is* my house and I'll do as I like here." As if to demonstrate, he wipes his shoes on the newspaper.

"When it gets dirty, I pull it up and put more down. Saves on sweeping."

"It's that hard to sweep?" I ask.

Before he can answer, Della's big car rounds the house. She's back, bringing a stack of bed stuff with her.

She carries them inside, sees the newspaper, and shakes her head. "Peavey, you are the most stubborn man I know." She sidesteps the soil from his shoes. "That's enough to make you go off your feed. Come on, Eddie."

I follow her into the dead great-grandparents' bedroom. She pulls the covers off the bed, folds them, and puts them in the closet.

"I brought a set of sheets and a blanket my grandsons use when they visit. They have Star Wars on them and that's probably a little young for your taste, but they're clean."

I reach for a corner to help, but she gives the bottom sheet a flip and begins tucking like she's done this a thousand times—which she probably has, I guess.

She hands me a pillow and a pillowcase. "You can help with this."

I try, but the pillow looks about three sizes bigger than

the pillowcase. I always thought I was a help to Mom, but I guess I never changed the sheets on my bed.

When I finally wrestle the pillow into place, Della goes over to the dresser, opens a drawer, and stuffs all the old pictures into it. She rearranges a few drawers, emptying two.

"These are for your clothes. You can put your own things on the dresser to make it feel like home."

I look around at the faded wallpaper and old, prissy curtains.

She puts her arm on my shoulder. "Eddie, have you ever stayed in that fancy hotel your mom works at? I mean, overnight?"

"No," I say. "But I want to someday."

"And do you think they'll get you a new mattress and paint the walls your favorite color when you stay?"

I laugh at that. "No!"

"Well, then, think of this as a hotel. You'll have clean sheets and room for your things, but you won't be the first person to sleep here."

"Okay," I say. "I can do that."

"And I know how a kid's mind works. Nobody died in this room that I know of, and I've been around for a long time."

Wow, I think, *she's good.* I didn't even realize that was bothering me, but I feel a whole lot better now.

I follow her back into the kitchen. "Eddie, you best get your shower. Peavey is taking you to town. Right, Peavey?"

She gives him a look like he's a little kid. He does that

Egyptian head slide again and says, "I said I would, Ordella, didn't I?"

"Just makin' sure, Peavey," she says as she leaves. "Just makin' sure."

After my shower, I unpack my clothes in the drawers Della emptied. I didn't bring anything from home to set on the dresser, but I put my pack of gum there, even though it's dirty from Ronnie's heel. I'm starting to feel as if I'm in a normal place, after all. Then I walk into the kitchen and step on the newspaper.

I find Peavey in the barn. "Get in the truck," he says. Not like an order, but not like he wants to talk about it, either.

"Where are we going?"

"Ordella seems to think a growing boy needs things that I don't have, so we're going to fix that."

Go, Della.

"Like what?"

"Milk, vegetables, whatever growing boys eat."

Peavey drives downtown.

"First off, I promised to take you to the library," he says, and I feel a wave of warmth toward the old guy. Well, at least a ripple.

Inside, a bunch of men with little kids are sitting on the floor, which seems kind of odd. I expect to see moms, but then I don't have that much experience with dads. A small feeling of emptiness comes over me. It's not homesickness, exactly. It's more for the dad stuff I'll never have.

The one woman there jumps up and comes over. Her name tag says CHERYL, LIBRARIAN.

"Hello, Peavey!"

He nods. "This here is my nephew, Ed."

"Well, goodness." She looks a little flustered. "I know the flyer said it was okay to bring an uncle or grandfather if your dad can't make it, but I guess I also should have put an age limit on the kids in the program. You're welcome to stay, of course, it's just that the other children are toddlers."

Peavey eyes the group sitting on the floor. Personally, I want the floor to swallow me up.

"It appears we caught you at a bad time, Cheryl. Ed's visiting and I promised him I'd get him set up on the computers here. We're not interested in any kind of kiddie party."

She laughs and seems to relax a little. "To tell you the truth, Peavey, this is the first Saturday of Donuts with Dads. Erma's off sick, and Joseph and I are running ourselves ragged."

Peavey holds up his hand. "Say no more. We'll come back."

"Wait." She fishes out a blue paper and hands it to him. "Just fill this out and bring it when you do. It's a permission form that you have to sign."

She looks at me. "Come back later, Ed. Joseph will still be here, and he'll show you around the library. All the boys like him."

"Okay," I say, deciding she's not so bad. Then she rushes over because one of the kids has spilled milk all over the carpet *and* one of the dads.

"Guess we picked a bad time," I say, climbing into the truck.

"There'll be others." Peavey pulls out onto the road and heads toward the store.

"It would appear everyone in Sheldon is shopping today," he says.

"You should come to Chicago if you think this is busy."

He drives twice around the main block downtown trying to find a parking place at the grocery store, finally pulling into an empty spot.

He yanks a cart out of the cluster at the store's entrance, then loads a bag of fertilizer from the pile in front of the store onto the bottom of the cart. He pushes it inside. I walk beside him past the condiments, approaching the produce, when he says, "Ordella said you'd be needing fruit."

"Okay." I look around. "What should I get?"

"Just get whatever you like to eat, I guess."

I grab a bag of golden delicious apples and a bunch of bananas.

"Anything else?"

"Um, grapes?" I say. He nods. I get the grapes, red seedless, and put them in the cart. "Okay, what next?"

"Well, she said to check if you brought toothpaste and deodorant."

"What is it with women and deodorant, anyway?"

Peavey chuckles.

"Yeah, I brought some. My mom wouldn't have let me leave without it."

"Then I reckon we just go up and down a few aisles. If you see something you like, put it in the cart here."

Mom shops with a list and there's not a lot of money for extras, so I've learned not to ask. But Peavey tosses in a couple of cans of chewing tobacco and a magazine about trucks. I pick up a can of ravioli and, when he doesn't even blink, I grab an extra. Next thing I know, we've got a cart full of food. Good stuff, like Twinkies, Pop-Tarts, and Pizza Rolls. Even a 24-pack of Coke.

After we load the bags into the truck, Peavey says, "We've got a stop to make before we go home. I'll be quick about it."

And he is. One thing about living in a small town, everything's close. Peavey pulls up in front of a big house and gets out.

"Make yourself useful, Ed. There's a bag of fertilizer in the back."

Great. Even a city kid knows what fertilizer is made of.

I grab the bag and follow Peavey as he limps to the front door. He takes off his cap when an old, gray-haired lady answers.

"Louise," Peavey says.

"Peavey! I wasn't expecting you." She pats her hair. "Why, I must look a mess."

"We're out running errands and I didn't think to call. Thing is, your grass has been looking a mite peaked and I had some spare fertilizer at home. Bought too much for my yard. I'd like to leave it here and spread it later."

"Oh, well, if you think the lawn needs it, Peavey," she says.

"I do."

"Can't you use it another time? I hate to take yours."

"No, it's best to use it up now before it goes bad," he says.

"You're so kind. Always thinking of others. Would you like to come in for a cup of coffee? And I have some carrot cake left that you're so fond of."

"No, got to be going. By the way, this here is my nephew, Ed."

We both say hello, and Louise says, "You may put that behind a bush, young man."

Whoa. What a change from the way she's sucking up to Peavey. You'd think I'm her servant, but I'm grateful to set the bag down.

"Well, thank you," she says to Peavey.

"You're welcome," he answers. "And I'll come back today to mow, if that's all right with you."

"That's just fine, Peavey." She gives him a big smile.

He nods, puts his cap back on, and gets in the truck. He doesn't offer any explanation about lying to the woman, so I don't ask. But when we get home and lift the sacks out of the truck, I change my mind.

"Peavey, I wasn't trying to listen, but I heard what you said to that lady. You didn't buy fertilizer for yourself, and how can processed manure 'go bad'?"

"I'm not normally in the habit of lying." He grabs two grocery bags. "I've known Louise Murray a long time. She's widowed and I mow her grass, but she insists on paying me. Five dollars every time."

"Five dollars! That's nothing." Even with money being short like it is at home, I know that much.

71

"Maybe not, but it is to her. So I take it because her pride is mighty. Then I find a way to give it back to her each time."

We set our bags on the kitchen table. "Fertilizer this week; next week I might drop by with a bag of oranges. She pays me for work done and I feel good about helping take care of her. It's a nice arrangement. Now let's get this stuff put away. We've got work to do."

I look at the food spilling out of the bags. "I'll do it." Putting groceries away is something I'm used to. Who knows what weird job awaits me in the barn?

Peavey seems relieved. "Then I'll go on over to Louise's and mow." He limps out to the barn. I get everything put away, feeling kind of guilty because the magazine and tobacco are the only things here that are for him. He's spent a lot of money for me to have the stuff I like to eat. Then I remember that Della forced him, and I stop feeling so bad.

After I fold up the sacks, I start to go to the barn, but wonder if Erin works on Saturdays. I run into my room and pocket a dollar, check in the mirror to see if my hair is sticking up, run my hand over the top, then take a whiff of my shirt.

I hurry to Kelley's, but slow down and walk inside as nonchalant as possible. Erin has a box of candy on the floor. She reaches for a bag and stretches high to slide it onto a display peg. My legs feel weak. I have to look away.

"Oh, hi!" she says, all perky. "You were in here yesterday."

I nod, afraid my voice will sound nervous.

"I'm Erin," she says, and then I have to answer.

"I'm Eddie." I sound almost normal.

"My sister told me you're staying with Peavey." She bends over to get another bag of candy.

"Here, let me help." I grab the whole box so she doesn't have to stretch so far, which makes no sense because seeing her stretch is something I'd like to watch all day.

"Thanks!" She reaches into the box and looks at me. A lock of purple hair hangs over one eye. "You're very nice."

I grin, bigger than I ever have. I look down because I can't look right at her without that stupid grin. I smell her perfume. I don't know what it's called, but I'll know that scent for the rest of my life.

When she finishes, she takes the box from me and balances it on her hip. The small star on her navel catches light when she moves. A saying from when I was little pops into my head. *Star light, star bright. First star I see tonight. I wish I may, I wish . . .* Oh, jeez.

"How long will you be staying?" she asks.

I tear my eyes away from the star. "A month."

She cocks her head to the side, like she's puzzled. "School starts in two weeks. Are you homeschooled?"

"No, I go to year-round school."

"Really? You'll have to tell me how that works."

I start to open my mouth when something flies out of nowhere and lands *thunk* in the box she's holding, causing both Erin and me to jump. I look down at a small purple purse.

Ronnie is standing at the end of the aisle.

"Oh, *nice*, Veronica!" Erin says.

"Next time you forget something, Erin Fielding, it's *too bad*. I'm not your slave."

"I didn't call you. I called Mom."

"Yeah, well, guess what? She's got clinic today. Big surprise!" Ronnie turns to me. "Hey there, Mr. Big City, are you helping us? Peavey said you'd be an extra set of hands, but I haven't seen you do anything yet."

"I—yeah, I'll be right there." My face is so hot it feels like it's going to ignite.

"Then hurry up!" She must have some kind of spidey-sense because she backs up and, without looking, stops just as she reaches the door. She raises her boot and kicks back to open it, spins, and leaves without ever touching the door.

"Just ignore her," Erin says. "She's *impossible*."

"I—" I point to the door, walking toward it. "I gotta go." I turn and smash my face right into the glass.

8

I'm outside, holding my wet nose, not knowing if it's blood or snot. It hurts, that much I know. The only good thing is Ronnie didn't see it. She's heading for the barn, so I hurry past to the house.

"What's with you?" she yells at my back. "I *said* we need help!"

"Be right dere," I say through my broken nose.

I run inside, fill the bathroom sink with cold water, and plunge my face into the sink bowl. When I finally look in the mirror, I look the same as I do when I have a cold, no worse than that. No blood. I know I can face Ronnie looking like this, but I'll never be able to see Erin again. Not after a colossal screw-up like walking into a freakin' door.

I hate myself for being such a loser and want to call my mom. I dry my face on the towel and make myself go to the barn. I won't be a baby and call Mom just because I made a fool of myself in front of the girl I like. I remind myself that if Mom hadn't sent me here it wouldn't have happened, and the longing to call her takes a hike.

Inside the barn is a big green tractor that wasn't there yesterday.

I try to keep my back to Ronnie. "I thought Peavey repaired lawn mowers. This looks awfully big."

"It *is* big, City. It's a John Deere tractor. Next weekend is Sheldon's Sweet Corn Festival. We'll be tuning up a lot of tractors because they pull the floats for the parade."

"You're joking, right? A festival about corn?" I can't help laughing, but stop the minute Ronnie throws a rag at me.

"Hey! Watch it!"

"*You* watch it. We live close enough to your stomping grounds to hear about the Taste of Chicago and all that stuff. It's no different here."

"Yeah, well, I beg to differ. We don't have 'floats' to celebrate certain food types."

"I'm not wasting my time talking to you. I've got work to do," she says. "Peavey said you'd help. Either do it or leave."

"Okay, okay. What do you need me to do?"

"You can start with something simple." She points to a lawn mower. "Tighten the lug nuts."

I examine the lawn mower, wondering what part of it is a lug nut. I look it over thinking I'll get a clue, but I can't tell what they've been working on or what needs work.

"You *do* know what a lug nut is, right?" she says in a tone I've come to hate.

"I do," I lie. "I'm not sure where they are on this particular lawn mower, though."

Ronnie cocks her head and looks at me for a minute. "Tell you what, City. Forget that. Why don't you run to the hardware store? It's three blocks west. Tell them you want to buy a left-handed wrench. Just charge it to Peavey's account."

"Okay," I say, glad to be getting away from her.

I meet Peavey on his lawn mower in the driveway.

"Going somewhere, Ed?"

"Ronnie sent me to the hardware store for a left-handed wrench."

Peavey shakes his head. "Looks like we need to have a talk with Ronnie. Come with me." He climbs off the mower.

Ronnie is doubled over, staggering with laughter, when we walk into the barn. Peavey says, "Ronnie, I think you owe Ed an apology."

She holds up one finger, like she needs a minute to catch her breath, then says, "Sorry you're so *stupid*, City!" She cracks herself up laughing again.

"What?" I ask.

"Ed, it's a joke to send a greenhorn to the store for a left-handed wrench. They get made a fool of not only by the person who sends them, but by the store when they ask for it."

I'm not sure what a greenhorn is, but I guess it must be an idiot.

"Ronnie," Peavey says, "I'm disappointed."

"But, Peavey"—she wipes tears from her eyes—"he didn't know what a lug nut was! A *lug nut*, Peavey!"

I walk out. I'm embarrassed to go to Kelley's and I can't go home.

I slowly shuffle myself toward the house when I realize

Peavey is close behind. "So you're going to tuck tail and run, is that it? Lindy's been calling me since you were a tiny mite telling me about you."

I slow down.

"The boy she talked about was smart and nice. Made me real proud."

I stop walking because I've never had a guy say that about me before.

"You know, Ed, it's not your fault you don't have a dad to teach you these things."

It's the first time someone other than me has brought up the fact that I don't have a dad.

"Yeah, well, why *don't* I have a dad, Peavey? No one says anything about him."

He takes a deep breath and I think he's gonna tell me. Instead he says, "That's a question for your mom, not me. But I'll tell you this: fathering a baby doesn't make a dad. Picking a boy up when he falls, being there when times are tough. That's what matters."

He's just like Mom, evading my question. I kick the rocks in the driveway so hard, pebbles scatter into the grass.

"Ed, your grandpa Emery loved you. He died of the cancer when you were little, so you might not know that. And he would've shown you things a boy oughta know. He'd want me to teach you and I will."

I hear him, but it all boils down to this. Because my real father didn't stick around, he doesn't matter to Peavey or my mom, so he's not supposed to matter to me. But he does.

And my grandpa would have been there for me, but he died, leaving me stuck with Peavey.

"As for Ronnie," Peavey says, "she should have a little more compassion."

Thinking of Ronnie makes me mad. Or maybe I'm just mad at everything and need someone to take it out on. "What's her problem, anyway? She's such a brat. I don't even know her and it's like she hates me."

"Aw, she doesn't hate you. Her parents are busy folks, both of them doctors, so she comes here. She's had the run of the place. I need to talk to her about this. Say, I know you've been itching to get to the library. Why don't you grab that blue form from the kitchen and run on over there."

"Okay." I try to keep my mad voice, but it's hard, since going to the library sounds great.

"When you get back, it's time you had a few lessons on machinery. Oh, and a lug nut? That's what holds on a tire."

I hate to ask, but I need to know. "And a left-handed wrench?"

"It's like asking for a left-handed pencil. No such thing."

I walk to the library, still amazed at how close everything is in this town. I make it in no time flat. Inside, I see Cheryl scanning books at the desk.

"Hey, there! Ed, isn't it?"

"Eddie."

"Eddie, sorry. It was a zoo when you were here this morning."

"That's okay."

She turns to a guy using the computer behind the desk. "Joseph, we've got a new patron. His name is Eddie."

Joseph looks to be about twenty, probably a college student.

"Hey, Eddie," he says. "You just move to town?"

"Nah, I'm staying with my uncle, Peavey McCall, for a few weeks."

"Cool. I like Peavey."

"Yeah, well, he signed this form."

Joseph takes it. "You need to sign it, too. Did you read it?"

"Um, no."

"Read it. It's an agreement that you can only be on the computers for one hour at a time and that you won't go to any inappropriate sites or chats, or IM anyone."

He hands me a pen. I read the agreement and hesitate over the words "inappropriate sites," wondering if *Matches-forTeens* is one. I decide it's not. I mean, it's just for dating. I sign my name.

"Follow me." He takes me around the library. He seems cool, and it's nice to have a guy show me around. It makes me realize how much I miss Whip.

"You a *SmackDown* fan?" he asks. I shake my head.

"No? I can't believe it." He stops by the DVD display. "How about *The A-Team*? You watch those reruns?"

Again, I shake my head.

"You're a tough nut to crack. What about graphic novels?"

"Yeah, they're okay." I say.

"Okay? They're fantastic!" He shows me a huge display of them. "These are my babies. Cheryl lets me order them. Anything you like but don't see, just ask."

"No, these are fine," I say, and pick up a few to check out. They *are* okay, but it's the bank of computers I'm waiting for.

He smiles at my selection of books, then takes me to the computers. "Here ya go. Just keep your nose clean. You've got an hour."

"Okay."

He walks away, and I smile at the screen for a minute. It's weird sitting at one of these and not feeling like I'm doing something wrong. I click on free_email.com, put in my user name and password, then find I have five e-mails.

I open the first one, which is from Whip.

Dude, u won't believe this but ur mom was nice 2 me. She thanked me 4 telling her u got there ok & all. So, spill. What's the old guy like?

The second one is from him, too.

U dead? Why haven't u emailed?

The next two are spam, but the last one is from a girl through *MatchesforTeens* named HotT. I click on it immediately.

Saw U on MatchesforTeens. U sound cute. Check out my site there.

Oh, jeez. My hands are sweating. I wipe them on my jeans, then click her link. HotT's user name should be UglE.

81

I mean, serious dog here. I decide not to answer but, hey, that was two girls and I hadn't even posted a picture! I decide to come by the library every day and see if anyone else contacts me. I e-mail Whip, which takes longer than I think it will because I'm trying to use the shortcuts that he and HotT used. It would probably be faster for me to just type, but it wouldn't look as cool.

`Thanx for telling my mom.`

I try to think of something to say.

`Old man isn't loaded. Doesn't even own a computer. I'm emailing from library. Town is small. This stinx. More l8r.`

I log off then check out my books at the desk.

"See ya 'round!" Joseph says as I leave.

Oh, yeah. Definitely.

Ronnie looks sheepish when I walk into the barn. Peavey shows me a tire iron and how to put it on a lug nut to tighten it. Ronnie never apologizes, but she's not laughing. I'm on the fourth wheel and feeling good about it when I look out the window and see Erin stepping out of Kelley's store. She looks so awesome. Then I remember walking into the door and know I'll never be able to face her again. Still, I watch. She pulls her purse strap up over her shoulder, and she's carrying a sack. She walks toward the barn! I step behind the John Deere so she won't see me.

"Ronnie!" she calls.

Ronnie doesn't hear her, so Erin yells louder, "Veronica Fielding!"

Ronnie looks up, startled. Her surprise turns to anger. "What?" she yells.

"Dad called and wants us home! Mrs. Daly died this morning."

"She did? Well, she was old and ornery."

Peavey quickly looks at me like he's thinking real hard. I don't know why, because I don't know any Mrs. Daly. Oh, yeah, she's the sick lady Della mentioned.

"I know that," Erin says. "But her son and his family are coming in today and Dad wants us home for dinner. We're having them over."

"How come?" Ronnie puts her hands on her hips.

"They're from out of town and they've just suffered a loss," Erin says.

"If they think they've suffered, they should have had to live next door to her," Ronnie mutters as she walks out the door.

Erin hands the sack to Peavey. "Poor Eddie got hurt at the store. Will you give him this from me and tell him I hope he feels better soon?"

My heart thumps. I want to hit rewind to hear that part again.

Peavey says, "You can give it to him yourself." He looks at me and I'm shaking my head as hard as I can. He clears his throat. "I mean, I'll see he gets it."

"Thanks." She smiles that incredible smile and walks out to where Ronnie is waiting.

Once they're gone, I jump out from behind the John Deere and grab the sack. Inside is one of those strip packages that holds ten packs of gum. Big Red. The same kind I bought there before. She remembered.

Peavey squints at me. "How did you get hurt at the store, Ed?"

"It was nothing." I'd walk into the door again, break my face if I had to.

Peavey and I start to clean up. He does, that is. I sort of wander around the barn in an Erin-induced fog. Then Della shows up at the door.

"Peavey?" she calls.

"Over here," he answers.

"I just heard that Arnetta Daly died."

"I know. Just a minute." He turns to me. "Ed?"

"Oh! Eddie, I didn't see you." Ordella throws her hand to her chest as if seeing me there scared her.

"Hi, Della."

Peavey clears his throat. "No sense in you hanging around here, Ed. I'd say we've done all the damage we can for one day."

"Okay." Then I gather my courage and ask, "Peavey, is it all right with you if I call home?"

"I think that's a real smart thing to do. And . . ." He takes off his cap and scratches his bald head.

"And what?"

"Well, I was thinkin' I might like to talk to Lindy myself." He looks at Della. She shrugs. He puts his hat back on. "You know what? I think I'll chat a spell with Ordella Mae, first. Tell your mom I said hello."

"Okay." I feel relieved that he decided not to talk to

Mom because I'm not calling her. I need to talk to Whip about Erin.

"Oh, man, she *wants* you!" Whip says when I get to the part about the package of gum.

"Maybe she's just being nice," I say, hoping he'll tell me I'm wrong.

"Dude! She's done all but ask you out!" he says. "First Stormy, then the other chick who e-mailed you, and now this Erin babe. You've got 'em chasing you!"

I figure that's going a little too far. Still, I feel good because I want to believe him. I also like that he's impressed.

"So what are you gonna do about it?" he asks.

Good question.

"I'm not sure," I say. "What would you do?"

He makes smooching noises into the phone. I hold it away from my ear, then yell into it, "Knock it off! I'm serious."

"So am I." He laughs.

"I could use some real advice, man," I say. "The thing is, I've never been on a date."

"Like I have?"

"No, but how about your dad? He dates girls all the time. Why don't you get some pointers from him. Like, how would I word it if I wanted to ask her out, or where would I take her, stuff like that."

"I don't know. He's kinda busy and . . . he's an old guy, anyway. What would he know?"

"What would he know? Jeez, Whip! He's juggling one

girlfriend on Tuesdays and another on Wednesdays! Your dad's like the king of dating."

"Oh . . . yeah." He coughs. "Well . . . I'll see what I can find out. I can't promise anything, though. Hey, this Erin, she got any sisters?"

I think of Ronnie. "Sort of."

"What? Like a stepsister?"

"No, like a pain-in-the-butt sister who's not cute *or* nice *or* remotely feminine."

"Think you could fix us up?"

"Are you deaf?"

"Not deaf. Hard up. If she's got a pulse, I'd take her out."

I laugh.

"You've had three girls after you in one week. The score is Professor, three; Whip, zip. But then, you having more than me is nothing new, is it?"

There's a tone in Whip's voice I never noticed before. It's like he's trying to tease but falling short.

"Huh?"

"Aw, nothing," he says.

But I wonder. Whip has practically everything that I want, so what does he mean? "No, really, tell me what you meant by that."

"I'm not even sure what I said. Oh, before I forget, you need to call your mom. She misses you."

I tense. "Then she shouldn't have sent me away."

"Still. Call her."

"She didn't want me under your 'bad influence.' Did you forget that part? Why do you care, anyway?"

"I've seen her in the hall. She looks lonely, Eddie."

"I've gotta go. Peavey's coming." It's not true, but I don't want the hardness I feel toward my mom to go soft.

"IM me later and let me know what you're gonna do about the hot chick."

"The library doesn't allow IMing, and Peavey doesn't have a computer, moron."

"I thought he was loaded," he says, and that makes me mad. As much as I like Whip, he always assumes things and never listens to how they really are.

"Gotta go." I hang up before I say something I'll regret. Right now, Whip is the only person I've got at home that I can still talk to.

9

Sunday comes and Kelley's is closed. I'm used to Chicago, where you can go almost anywhere at any time and find something open. Not here in Sheldon. I'd even welcome the diversion of Ronnie, which tells you how boring a day alone with Peavey can be.

Then Louise walks up to the house wearing a flowery dress and high heels, and carrying the biggest purse I've ever seen. What's worse is that she's got so much perfume on I can almost see a cloud around her. Still, I'm glad for a break in the monotony.

"I've come to pay you for mowing, Peavey. You're always so good about taking care of me. I don't want you to have to wait for your money."

But she's so cheap! It's the longest minute of my life when she hands him a ten-dollar bill and waits while he fishes around, trying to find five bucks to give her in change. I want to run to my room and give her the money myself, just to end the embarrassment.

After she leaves, Mom calls. Peavey answers the phone, and I can tell it's her by the way he's talking. I think about sneaking out the back door. Instead I wait in the recliner because I know he'll put me on.

"Well, he hasn't changed much since you talked to him yesterday," Peavey says. I cringe and sink lower in the seat because now he knows I didn't call her.

"I see." He turns to look at me. "Well, I'll let you have him in a second. I probably should talk to you. That is, Ordella Mae and I had a talk yesterday, more like an argument and, well . . . Eddie's here now, so I'll just let you talk to him. You and I can have a go later. No, no, everything's okay. Here he is."

He holds the phone out. I take a deep breath, get out of the recliner, and grab it. Peavey goes outside.

"Hello."

"Hi, stranger. Guess you're still pretty mad if you lied to Peavey about talking to me."

"I didn't lie." Another lie. "I changed my mind."

"So," she says, and then hesitates.

I stay quiet.

She clears her throat. "Ahoy, matey."

When I was little and Mom was mad at me, I would bring this stuffed parrot from my room. I'd hide behind a chair, put the parrot up where she could see it, and say, "Ahoy, matey." It always made her laugh and she got over being angry.

"It doesn't work as well without the parrot," I say.

"Ah. I'll remember that."

But hearing her voice causes a pain in my stomach as sharp as a toothache. That's the bad thing about being mad at Mom. Every memory I have has her in it.

"So . . . how's the Hilltop?"

"Okay," she says. "How are things there?"

I think about missing home, Peavey and his weird habits, and Ronnie.

"Awful."

"Awful?" She asks this like it's a shock. "How?"

"What do you mean how? You lived here." Despite missing her, I'm getting mad again. "You've gotta know there's nothing to do. Nothing's familiar. The people aren't nice." Okay, another sort of lie, but I'm on a roll. "I've got no friends. It's like prison."

"Eddie, I think you're exaggerating."

I snort, mainly because she hates that sound. "If it's so great, how come you never came back?"

"Who has time? You know how busy I am with work and school."

"You didn't always go to school, Mom. You used to have more time. We've never visited here."

She sighs. "I guess I'm just not a small-town person."

"Oh, I get it. It's not good enough for you to visit, but it's a great place to send your only son to *live* for a month!"

"Eddie, listen to me. I've had time to cool off and realize I was hasty in sending you there. And maybe it's not right that Peavey visits us, but we never visit him. When you get back, we'll talk about all that. But for now, I know Peavey and Della and I'm confident that they're taking good care of you."

I'm too mad to think about whether this is true. All I hear is that once again she's making all the calls that affect me.

"I've gotta go," I say.

"Wait! Let me talk to Peavey."

"Can't. He left." Well, he's messing around the yard, but technically he did leave the house.

"I'll call back soon," she says.

"Whatever. Bye." I hang up, not waiting for her to say goodbye, too. It's a satisfying feeling. For about ten seconds. Then I wish I hadn't been so nasty.

Peavey comes in. It must be pretty obvious that I'm in a black mood because he asks, "Something bothering you?"

I think of all the ways I could answer that, but I complain about what bothers me the least. "I miss playing basketball."

Finally, the day ends—along with the last of Della's noodles—and I go to sleep by pushing Mom out of my head and filling it with Erin instead. She surely must like me to buy that gum for me. Maybe she thought walking into the door was charming rather than stupid. I try to think of something cool to do for Erin tomorrow.

Monday morning I'm up and dressed before Peavey. I want to take Erin something, anything, to thank her for the gum and to show her how much I like her. I finally decide to go with nothing. Dumb, I know, but I figure if I go just to be with her, it might mean something special.

After a quiet breakfast of doughnuts and milk, I give my underarms a double blast of deodorant and head over to Kelley's.

I hear Erin's tinkling laugh before I see her. When I do, my breath catches. She's bent over the counter, her chin resting in her hands, looking incredible. Then I see she's talking to a guy and my feet go numb. I stand frozen until she looks up.

"Eddie! Come meet Isaac Daly. He's visiting."

I nod at this dude who is a good six inches taller than I am and, judging by the soul patch below his lip, has been shaving for a while.

"Isaac, this is Eddie. He's visiting, too." She laughs again. Funny how that sound sort of grates on me now.

Isaac doesn't smile and barely looks my way. " 'Sup?" he says.

I ignore him and turn to Erin. I start to thank her for the gum yesterday, but she's looking at him, not me. I wonder if she even remembers yesterday.

She finally tears her eyes away from him and asks me, in what now sounds like official salesperson speak, "Can I get you anything?"

Before I answer, she says, "Wow! I just realized how much you two resemble each other. Through the eyes, anyway."

I look at him and don't see it. He has long brown hair

and is a couple of years older. We both have blue eyes, but big deal.

"Are you related?" she asks.

I find my voice. "I think Peavey is my only relative."

"You're the only person here that I know," he says to her, and she goes all soft and dreamy-looking. It's a look I've never gotten.

I want to get out of here, so I say, "Speaking of Peavey, he needs me. I've got to go. See ya."

There's no "Wait, Eddie, why are you here?" Not even a "See ya" back. She's totally locked onto this Isaac dude. I make sure to open the door this time, but it wouldn't matter. She'd never notice if I walked through the glass.

Outside the store I feel like the world just got knocked sideways by a meteor and wonder how I can feel so bad now, when I felt so great ten minutes ago. Before I can shake the feeling, if that's even possible, Della's car flies around the corner, stopping hard at Peavey's. I hope I never have to ride with her, but I'm glad to see her and open her door before she gets the seat belt off.

"Good morning, Eddie!" she says, flicking her cigarette butt past me. She gives me a hug. And because I lost something important but I'm not sure what, I hug her back, not wanting to let go. She pats my arm. "I brought meat loaf today. Think you can help me carry it in?"

"Sure." I grab the pan from the backseat. Meat loaf's not my favorite, but I don't think I'll ever feel like eating again, anyway.

Della looks around the kitchen. Obviously, Peavey was

busy while I was gone, gathering the old, dirty newspapers off the floor and spreading new ones. Della shakes her head, then turns to me. "So, how's the old man treating you?"

"Okay," I say. "Good."

"Are you making your mom proud by keeping your washing up?"

"I'm not out of clean clothes yet."

"Just make sure you do," she says. "How's everything else?"

"Fine." I don't meet her eyes.

Della sighs. "I raised three boys, so I know you're probably not going to tell me if something's bothering you. But you can, you know."

I think of telling her about Erin, but what would I say? I'm not even sure why I feel this bad, so putting it into words is more than I can manage.

"No, really, everything's great."

"Well, I'm sure Peavey is a little different from what you're used to."

If she wants to think Peavey is bothering me, I'll let her. It's true that he does, about fifteen times a day, so it's not a stretch.

Della rearranges the fridge to make room for the meat loaf. "Thing is, he had polio when he was little."

"He did?" I say. "I didn't know that."

"Surely you know by now he's not one to talk about himself."

She pushes the Coke cans aside, shaking her head. "I see you made all kinds of healthy choices at the store."

I don't answer, and she goes on. "He didn't have too bad a case, but it was enough to make him fall behind in school. He was always shy and that made it worse. His brother, Emery, and my husband, Arthur, took him under their wings, so to speak, so Peavey never really looked for other friends."

She closes the fridge door. "First Arthur died, then Emery. I look out for him some; Ronnie's good company. Now he has you."

She takes a deep breath. "I guess what I'm saying is he might seem a little odd, but circumstances made him that way. He's a good man."

"Okay," I say, because, really, what does she want me to say? Sorry he had polio and no friends, but someone should have shown the guy how to get a life? Or at the very least, how to do dishes?

"I need to get back to work," Della says.

I watch her leave, then I go to the barn. Ronnie looks up when I walk in. She doesn't speak, but she does raise her wrench—which is the closest she's come to saying hi.

Peavey asks if I'd rather sharpen blades or pick up the place. I choose cleaning, which I have the best chance of not screwing up. We work without talking, so I have a lot of time to think about Erin. *Is Isaac still there? Do I still stand a chance with her? Did I ever?* I think about calling Whip, but he wasn't any help before Isaac, so he'd probably be less now.

I must have been lost in thought for quite a while, because I'm surprised when Peavey says, "Time for lunch. You'd best run along, Ronnie."

She rises from behind a lawn mower and wipes her hands. "I don't want to."

"Now, Ronnie, your folks want you girls to keep the Daly kids company this afternoon while their parents make funeral arrangements. You know that."

"I don't know why we have to be so dang nice to them. I have to go to Mrs. Daly's wake tomorrow. And then the funeral after that! I didn't even like the old bat."

"Ronnie," Peavey says.

"Well, you're not going. Why do I have to? You've known her a lot longer than I have."

"A privilege of getting old," Peavey says. "Right now, though, your folks want you to be nice to their neighbor's family."

"Okay, okay." Ronnie puts her tools away. "But I'm not hanging around Isaac. Last night I had to sit across from him at dinner and I wanted to go like this"—Ronnie beats on the hood of the tractor—"Hello? Did you forget to pack your personality?"

"Really?" It's out before I know it.

Ronnie looks as surprised as I am that I'm talking to her. "Yeah, a total loser. When Erin gets past his good looks, she'll see."

She shouts over her shoulder, "Bye."

It could have been meant for Peavey. It probably was. But I call, "See ya later!" because she made me feel better about Erin. Plus, Ronnie said Isaac was good-looking. Erin said I resemble him. So that has to mean Ronnie thinks

I'm good-looking. I can't figure out why this matters, but it does. Maybe my ego just needs a shot, even if it's from Ronnie.

After lunch, a man pulls up in a tractor.

"Just change the oil and give her the once-over, Peavey," he says. "Don't want her to conk out while I'm pulling the quilting-bee float. I'd have twenty mad hens after me."

"Will do," Peavey says.

When the man leaves, Peavey shows me how to change the oil in a tractor. I wash my hands in the house afterward and head back to the barn. In the meantime, Louise has shown up, carrying a basket. She has on a straw hat that could provide enough shade for three people and a shirt with bumblebees and honeypots sewn all over it. Remembering all that perfume from before, I stay by the door.

"You must think I'm a noodle-head, Peavey." She pats his arm. "I just can't seem to remember how that newfangled handle you gave me last month works."

"Just push in the button on the handle and slip it into the trowel, like so." Peavey takes a handle that is about a foot long and slips it into a tiny shovel. A preschooler could have figured it out.

"What would I do without you, Peavey? I'll tell you what. Next time you mow my yard, I'll make a peach cobbler. It's my way of paying you back."

It occurs to me that Peavey ought to weigh three hundred pounds from old ladies cooking for him. He must like that, because he's always so nice to Louise. But it doesn't keep him from arguing with Della.

I don't want to interrupt and I definitely don't want to talk to Louise, so I slip back into the house until she leaves. Working on the tractor had kept my mind busy, but now I have time to think again about Erin flirting with Isaac.

I pick up the television remote to find a diversion. I surf, and there she is like an old friend—Oprah Winfrey. I don't know why her show is on in the afternoon here instead of in the morning like at home, but I take it as a sign and push back the recliner. She's yakking it up with some celebrity who has an eating disorder. Then everyday people come on, talking about their stuffed-barfed-starved lives—nothing to interest me. But Oprah gets them laughing when they're crying and acts like, well, like a mom to them. Sappy, I know, but for the rest of the hour I let myself buy into the warm feeling for the same reason I bought into the Easter Bunny after I was too old for it. Just because it made me feel good. I think of Mom and wonder if that's why she watches Oprah every day.

When the credits roll, I click off and flip the recliner into sitting position. I hear breathing. I look over my shoulder and see Peavey sitting at the kitchen table. I didn't even hear him come in, but he must have been there for a while.

"Now that"—he points to the television—"is one smart woman."

That night we have Della's meat loaf, which really is okay with enough ketchup on it. Top the meal off with an apple and a bag of chips and it's not bad at all. Peavey is at the point where he eats sitting instead of standing, but I'm still on my own as far as preparing my food and cleaning up.

I'm going at Della's roaster with Brillo when the phone rings. After the third ring, I grab it with a soapy hand, tucking it between my ear and shoulder as I work the pan.

"'Lo?"

"Ahoy, matey."

"Mom?" The slippery phone clanks onto the counter. I grab it, dry it off, and stick it back to my ear.

"I not only have the parrot here, I have a patch over one eye. Oh, and crackers! You know, for the parrot."

I hear her laugh. Talking to her again was the last thing I thought I wanted to do, but I was wrong.

"I tried to give you time to get over being mad at me, but I missed you too much."

"I'm glad you called."

"Then let's start over. Is there anything you like about Sheldon?"

"Well, it's small. Della is nice, though."

"Della! Oh, tell her hello for me."

"Okay."

"Oops!" says Mom. "That's okay, honey, it goes right up here."

I wonder who she's talking to, because it sure isn't me.

"Mom? Did you take up drinking?"

"No!" She laughs. "Whip just dropped a can. He's helping me put groceries away. I'll let you talk to him when we're through. Now, where was I? Oh, Della. Isn't she great?"

"Wait! Rewind." I must be hearing things. "Jared Sweeney is in our apartment. Without me."

"I'm here, too, Eddie," she says. "He's not alone."

I *have* to be hearing things.

"And you're calling him honey as if you like him," I say. "Wait! Rewind more. You called him Whip, right? The name I can't say without your eyebrows going all pointy and arrows shooting out your retinas?" I'm breathing as hard as if I've run two miles.

"Well, Jared came over last night to check on me. I was feeling blue, missing you, and he noticed. We talked. Why didn't you ever tell me you call him Whip because he loves Miracle Whip? It sounded like some gang-related name to me."

I may be a recent Oprah convert, but I've had years of listening to her show and, as I said before, I've picked up a few things. For instance, I can't help but notice that Mom has turned the conversation around so I'm on the defensive.

"Maybe I didn't tell you, *Boo*, because you didn't give me the chance *or*"—this just came to me and it's a good one—"trust that I might have decent taste in friends!"

"Oh, Eddie, let's not fight again. I miss you so much and—"

I don't let her finish. "Really? You don't sound lonely. And just so you know, there's nothing about home that I miss."

I hang up the phone and take my anger out on the pan, scrubbing until it gleams. I can't believe it. Mom and Whip. It's as if she just wants a boy around and any will do. If one doesn't work out, ship him off and bring in another. Maybe that's why I don't have a dad. She probably kicked him out when I was born. Only one male at a time needed. And the worst part is, I sent him to Mom.

Just as I'm rinsing off the last dish, the phone rings again. How many times is she going to call here? I'm not answering. After about the eighth ring, Peavey finally picks it up.

He holds the phone out to me. "It's a fella by the name of Sam Sweeney."

Mr. Sweeney? Why would he call? I grab the phone, thinking the worst. Mom has offed herself.

"Hello?"

"Hello, you stupid jerk."

"Whip? I thought it was your dad!"

"I said Sam Sweeney. I didn't lie. Jared Samuel Sweeney, that's me."

"Yeah, well, I'm busy here," I say. Whip is the second-to-last person I want to talk to right now, Mom being the last.

"No kidding? Me, too. I'm busy in my own apartment all by myself because your mom is crying at yours. She's so upset that I had to leave. So guess what? I don't give a crap that you're busy."

"Listen."

"No, you listen. You've got it all, Eddie. I act like I don't care. You've got the brains. I call you The Professor 'cause you're so smart. But did you ever think how it feels to be me? Left in the stupid class while you move up?"

"Hey!" I say, but he keeps going.

"You've got the reputation for being the good guy, the

one who's never in trouble. You've got a *mom*, Eddie. And me, I act like none of it bothers me, but it does. And you know what? I always thought if your mom started liking me just a little, you'd be happy. But instead you ruin that for me. Oh, and one more thing—" *Slam!*

I hang up the phone, breathing hard. The mound of bubbles in the sink gently moves. I take my hand and swipe them. They blow across the room to where Peavey stands, eyes blinking behind his too-big glasses.

I can't deal with him. Not now.

I go outside and sit on the back step. I never see this much sky where I live, and the hugeness of it makes me feel smaller and more lost than I've ever felt.

How can Whip think I have it all? If he were here now, I'd smash his face.

Peavey comes outside. I let out a huff of air and look the other way, hoping he'll take the hint. It's not until I feel something roll to my side that I notice a new basketball.

"Don't have a hoop, but maybe you can toss it against the barn. If you've a mind to, that is."

I turn to him, but he's gone back inside. I grab the ball, pick a spot on the barn wall, and aim for it. I hit it the first time. I keep hitting it until my head clears and I feel like I take up my fair share of the universe again.

I put two slices of bread in the toaster and watch out the kitchen window for Erin to come to work. I'm thinking that maybe without Isaac around I'll get up the courage to go talk to her. She comes to work, all right, with Isaac driving what I hope is his parents' car. It's a red, restored Mustang convertible and it's a beauty. As if Isaac alone wasn't enough competition, he pulls up in such a cool car.

I'm glad it's a convertible, because I can see them and I know they aren't kissing. They sit in the car for a long time. Too long. But then, any time she spends with someone who isn't me would seem too long. Finally, Erin gets out and Isaac pulls away.

The phone rings and I get busy buttering toast at the kitchen counter. I don't want to answer in case it's Mom. If I could wish for one modern convenience in this prehistoric dwelling, it would be caller I.D.

Peavey picks it up. "No, that's all right, Ronnie. Well, I

understand it's not all right with you." He chuckles. "But it's fine that you're not coming today. You know that."

Ronnie's not coming? Funny, that should make me happy, but it just means another long day like Sunday, with nothing to ease the boredom.

"Well, they'll be gone soon. Do what your folks tell you now."

He hangs up.

"Ronnie's not coming?"

"No." He sits down. "It appears Erin had to go to work and someone needs to watch the youngest Daly children while their parents get ready for the wake."

"But that's nuts! Why can't Isaac do it? He's the brother."

"You'd think, wouldn't you?" Peavey finishes his coffee and carries his dishes to the sink. "Well, the apple doesn't fall far from the tree."

"What do you mean?"

Peavey looks startled. Like he didn't realize he'd said it out loud. "As I recall, his dad, Jeff, seemed to dodge responsibilities."

"Was Mrs. Daly as awful as Ronnie says?"

"The Dalys owned the hotel here. Being it was the only one in town, and in a historical building to boot, Arnetta Daly thought she was high society. She looked down on everyone and acted like her son could do no wrong. I guess you could say she made some enemies along the way."

"Ronnie's parents must have liked her."

"By the time they came to town, she was just a lonely old lady. Jeff and his family never visited much."

I finish my toast. Peavey stares out the window for a while, then says, "I thought they'd be gone by now, truth to tell. Seems like they're dragging this funeral out a bit."

"I don't know anything about funerals," I say, taking my plate and cup to the sink and washing them.

"I think I need to speak to Ordella about a thing or two." He thumps the table once with his knuckles, as if he's been debating but now it's settled. "Any place I can drop you off? No need for you to start work till I do."

I remember a line from an old movie: "In this one-horse town?" I mean, where would I go? Then I think of the library.

"Yeah! Actually, there is."

"I'll be back in about an hour," Peavey says. Perfect. An hour is all I can be on the computer, anyway.

I sign in for computer number four, wave to Joseph when he calls out, "Dude!" Then I log on and check my e-mail. There isn't even one, and I wonder, how can that be? I think maybe I should go to *MatchesforTeens* and add more info to my profile. After all, Whip didn't have time to do much work on it that day at my apartment.

I pull up the Web site and log in as The Professor. It says I'm sixteen. I forgot about that. I decide to leave it. Maybe those two girls wouldn't have clicked on it if they'd known I'm only thirteen. But if I lie about that, then I kind of have to lie about other things, like what grade I'm in. When I'm finished, I realize I don't even know this person who is supposed to be me. Then I wonder about girls like Stormy and HotT. Did they lie, too?

I randomly choose some girls and look at their profiles. They all sound good, which makes me suspicious. I mean, HotT sounded good until I saw her picture. So I click on their photo gallery. Some are cute, but not Erin-cute. That makes me want to stop looking at cyber babes and go see the real thing. But I remember she's with Isaac and keep clicking. Photo after photo pops up. One catches my eye: it's titled "Me and my budz." I expect to see a girl with her friends, which I do, one on each side of her. But all three girls are topless, smiling straight at the camera as if they're wearing their Sunday best.

I quickly look around. Fortunately, this part of the library is empty. I look back at the screen. Oh, man. I just don't get a sight like this every day.

The sign above me says PRINTING: TEN CENTS EACH FOR BLACK-AND-WHITE, FIFTY CENTS FOR COLOR.

I reach for my pocket and feel some change. Not much. I count it out. Thirty-three cents. I look back at the screen. I would *love* to have those beauties in color. Still, with thirty cents I can get three black-and-white copies. I could mail one to Whip. Who knows, I may even tell him I took the picture at a party here in Sheldon.

I laugh, thinking about his reaction. He'd be crazy jealous. So I choose black-and-white, scroll to three copies, and double-click on print.

I don't hear anything. Maybe their printer is quieter than Mom's. I look for it, but don't see it. I stand to see if the printer is on the desk behind the monitor. It's not.

Then I crawl under the desk. Nothing there, either. I stay

crouched to keep from banging my head and inch my way back out from under the desk, when I bump into two shoes that weren't there a minute ago.

This can't be good.

I poke my head out and see Joseph holding the "Me and my budz" printouts.

"Is this what you're looking for?"

My face flashes red-hot. I think my ears are gonna smoke and fall off. Nothing comes out of my mouth but short, fast breaths.

"The printers are at the front desk," he says.

Then the thought hits me. It's Joseph. He's just gonna laugh about this. One guy to another.

"I guess you caught me," I say. It's supposed to come out confident. Instead I sound like I'm seven.

"Looks like," he says.

I try again. "I didn't know. That the printers were up front."

"Oh, I was pretty sure of that," he says. I notice he still doesn't give me the pictures. Instead he reaches for the computer and closes the site. "I think you're done now."

And then I know that I'm more than done. I double-clicked for fun, but all I got is trouble.

I tell Joseph that Peavey will be back to pick me up at the end of my hour. In the meantime I scrunch low in the reference-section chair because it's the one place in the building people seem to ignore. Cheryl walks by, though, so I grab a book and open it, too embarrassed to talk.

Peavey comes and calls me to the desk. I put one heavy foot in front of the other. I feel as if I'm going before a judge. Joseph stands behind the desk. He hands Peavey an Incident Report. It's very official looking. I glance over Peavey's shoulder to read it. "Eddie McCall viewed inappropriate Web sites, proof attached." And the incriminating printout is stapled to it.

Joseph explains that the first offense gets a warning. The second time, I won't be able to use the computers for three months. Peavey tells him there won't be a second time. I agree. I'll never step foot in the place again.

Peavey doesn't look at me. He doesn't take the report. He thanks Joseph and we leave.

My body is so tense I think it might shatter if it gets bumped. Peavey doesn't say anything on the way home. Not that he's much of a talker but I want him to say something. I wonder if this is a form of punishment. His silence is worse than Mom's yelling.

We reach Peavey's and he gets out of the truck. I stay, too upset to move. Peavey takes off his hat, scratches his head, then puts his hat back on.

"Ed? You ever mowed?"

I shake my head.

"Then it's time you learned. I've got other things to do and the grass here is getting tall."

It's not. But at least he's speaking to me, so if he wants me to mow, I'll mow. I climb out of the truck.

He takes me to his riding lawn mower, explains about the

gear shift and how to raise, lower, and engage the mower deck. Then he goes inside the barn. I start the mower. After grinding the gears a few times, I get the hang of it. If today wasn't one of the worst days of my life, I would probably enjoy this. I mean, it's as close to driving a car as I've come.

After a while, I think about Joseph. I was so wrong to expect that he'd be a friend and not rat on me. But it wasn't really his fault. He was doing his job. As for Peavey, he took me to the library to have some fun and what did I do? I shamed him.

Then I think about how there's got to be something fundamentally wrong with me that I can't seem to stay away from those sites. Can I be a total pervert at the age of thirteen?

It seems like I just started mowing, so I'm surprised to see I've finished the yard. I pull the lawn mower into the barn and Peavey comes over.

"How'd it go?"

"Great! I mean, she handles well," I say, trying to sound like a man.

Peavey nods. "For someone who's never mowed before, you did good."

"Thanks." Even now Peavey is nice to me, which makes me feel worse.

"It's hot," he says. "Let's get us a couple of Cokes."

"I'll get them." I jump off the tractor and run inside, eager to try to convince him that I'm an okay person, even if I don't think I am.

109

When I come out, Peavey is sitting on the porch step. I hand him a soda and sit close by. I know I have to apologize and decide to jump in.

"Peavey, I'm sorry. I—"

He interrupts. "Did I ever tell you about the time I broke into Emery's stash?"

I blink. "Stash?"

"We shared a room, as you know. He was older and always messin' with stuff beneath his bed late at night. Then he'd take a flashlight under his blanket to look at it. I was just a snot-nosed kid and he wouldn't tell me what he was doin'. One day when he left with Arthur, I investigated. I just had to see for myself what was so interesting under that bed."

Peavey takes a drink. "Well, it was an old Monopoly box, but there was no game inside. No sir. Inside that box was a couple of *Playboy* magazines."

Aw, jeez. I *am* perverted. I inherited it from my grandpa.

"I looked through each one, seeing things I'd never seen before. Naturally, I lost track of time. Emery came home and caught me. He'd have thrashed me for sure if I hadn't threatened to tell our parents about those magazines."

Peavey chuckles. Then he gets serious. "Point is, it's natural to be curious. But here's something to think about. Those girls in the magazine and on the Internet, they're people with families. They're someone's daughter or sister. They could be someone's mom. Lord only knows why they've chosen to expose themselves like that."

Peavey stands and stretches his bum leg. Then he looks at me for the first time since he started talking. "One day you're gonna fall in love and maybe marry. You owe it to your lady and to yourself to have that part of your life be about you two without pictures of women you'll never meet filling up your head. Now that's all I'm gonna say on the subject."

He starts to walk away.

"Peavey, wait. Are you gonna tell my mom?"

"Why would I do that? Didn't I just say that's all I'm gonna say on the subject?"

"Well, yeah, but—"

"But nothing. Time's wastin' and we've got work to do."

Peavey *doesn't* say another word about it. He doesn't treat me badly, either. He acts like it never happened, and for the first time I'm grateful to be here instead of home. When Mom gets mad, she yammers at me, then leaves the room. But she gets worked up again and again and comes back each time with a new verbal assault. Being with Peavey definitely has an upside.

While we're working, I can't get Peavey out of my mind. I think about how he could easily call my mom, but he said he wouldn't. And I remember that Della had to tell him to take me shopping, but he bought me anything I wanted. He even bought me a basketball. I think about how he takes care of weird Louise, and how kind he is to Ronnie—which can't be easy.

That afternoon, I keep my head down and help Peavey. I figure I owe it to him, and he needs lots of help. The people of Sheldon take their sweet corn fest seriously. They've strung a banner across downtown announcing the dates, August 5–7, this coming Friday through Sunday. We get a regular line of big tractors that need to be cleaned up for the parade. I do whatever Peavey asks and don't once make fun of Sheldon's ode-to-corn floats—as much as I'd like to.

Later that evening, after Mrs. Daly's wake, Ronnie comes by to help. Mostly she complains.

"It's not fair. Erin didn't have to go because she had to work. It was just an excuse."

"Maybe not," Peavey said. "When you have a job you have a responsibility."

"Well, I have a job, don't I?" She gets in his face. "Don't I have a responsibility to help you?"

"Maybe your boss is nicer than Erin's," Peavey says, and winks at me when she turns away grumbling.

Before long the lights at Kelley's go out and I see Erin locking up. Peavey and Ronnie are busy, and I should be, too. But Erin looks so amazing as she waits outside for her ride that I'm drawn to the door of the barn, watching her.

"Hi, Eddie!" she says.

I'm grease-covered and should stay away, but her voice sends a signal to my feet. Next thing I know, I'm standing beside her.

"I haven't seen you all day," she says.

She noticed! "I've been busy helping Peavey."

"That's nice."

She turns her smile on me like a spotlight and I feel warmed by it.

"Is Veronica at Peavey's?" she asks.

"Yeah, she's there. Should I get her?"

"Maybe in a minute."

A tingle runs through me at the thought that she wants to stay and talk to me. I feel brave enough to say, "Maybe I could walk you home."

"Actually, I see my ride coming now."

I don't have to turn to know that it's a red Mustang convertible pulling up beside us. What does surprise me is that Isaac isn't driving.

"Hello, beautiful," this dude who must be Erin's dad says.

"Oh, Mr. Daly! Hi."

Mr. Daly? I thought he was *her* dad. I look at Erin and her face is flushed.

"Isaac mentioned he was picking you up. I had to get out of there, so I told him I'd get you." He loosens his tie. "Those wakes are murder."

He leans across and opens the door for her. "Hop in, sweetheart."

Something feels weird. I may not be around a lot of dads, but calling Erin "beautiful" and "sweetheart" just sounds wrong to me.

"Sure!" Ronnie says, appearing out of nowhere. She pushes past Erin and plops into the front seat. I don't know who is more surprised, me, Erin, or Mr. Daly, who clearly doesn't like this turn of events, judging by the look on his face.

"Get in the backseat, Erin," Ronnie says. "Or walk."

Mr. Daly says in a tight voice, "Veronica, I didn't know Isaac was taking you home, too."

Ronnie snorts. "Isaac didn't, either. But it's not every day I get to ride home in style. Erin can sit in the back, since she got out of the wake today." Ronnie holds the seat up as Erin climbs in. "Like you said, they're murder."

They drive off with Mr. Daly looking mad because Ronnie is in the car. Erin seems disappointed, probably because Prince Isaac didn't show. But Ronnie, with one arm sprawled across the seat and the other propped on the windowsill, is smiling like the queen of the corn parade.

Peavey comes up to me, squinting at the Mustang as it rounds a corner.

"Who was that?" he asks in a voice that's gruff for him.

"I guess it's Isaac's dad."

"*He* picked up those girls?"

"Yeah," I say. "I don't think he knew he was picking up Ronnie, though."

"What are you sayin'?"

"That he came for Erin. Ronnie sort of forced herself into the front seat."

The harsh look on his face softens until he looks at me. "Did he say anything to you?"

"No," I say. "I don't think he even noticed me. Why?"

He turns toward the house and doesn't answer me. When I come in, he's already on the phone.

"Just makin' sure you got home safe, Ronnie," he says. "Next time you girls need a ride, I'll take you."

He acts worried, and I finally say, "I guess Ronnie and Erin don't know it's dangerous getting into a stranger's car."

"Jeff Daly's no stranger," Peavey says. "Sometimes it's people you know that are the most dangerous."

He sits in his recliner, then asks, "Are you sure he didn't say anything to you?"

"Yeah, I'm sure." Then, because I can't shake the uneasy feeling I had with the guy, I say, "But he did say something weird to Erin. He pulled up and said, 'Hey, beautiful.' I know Mr. Daly was doing Isaac a favor by picking her up, but it seemed like a weird thing for a dad to say."

"It is." Peavey shook his head. "But just because you're someone's dad doesn't make you a good man."

Ronnie comes the next morning before the funeral to help. I make myself stay away from Kelley's, but it's hard. When Erin is alone, she's nice to me. But I know that if Isaac is there, it will be all about him. I could probably shoplift and get away with it, she's so into him.

I break down and ask Ronnie when the Dalys are going home.

"No clue," she says. "Not soon enough."

Peavey's head pops up from the other side of a tractor. "They'll go home right after the funeral, won't they?" he asks.

"Not all of 'em."

"All?" I ask. "How many are there?"

"There's Stuck-on-Himself Isaac. Stupid Micah, he's about eleven years old. Pain-in-the-Rump Leah, who's six. Then there's Anna, the mom." Ronnie struts around, sticking out her chest and patting her hair. I can't help smiling.

"What about . . . her husband?" Peavey asks.

"Big-Shot Jeff will stay a while. He's getting the house ready to sell."

Peavey doesn't answer, just blows that long one-note whistle—which I *hate*.

Della pulls up and I walk outside to wait for her. She's always nice and normal, except for her statement T-shirts. Today's says YARD SALES: THE FIRST RECYCLERS.

I open her car door and lift out a roast, which smells so good I almost drool onto the lid. Peavey comes limping out of the barn. "Ed, take that on in. I need a word with Ordella Mae."

"Sure." It's what I was going to do anyway.

I take the time to crack open a can of Coke and pinch off a hunk of the steaming roast. I blow on it and cram it into my mouth. *Heaven.* I sit down at the table.

Out the window I see Peavey and Della having what appears to be a serious conversation. Della lights up a cigarette. Peavey's arms start moving and he begins pacing, the most animated I've ever seen him. Della's voice gets louder. Peavey comes into the house and she follows.

They stop when they see me. I try to swallow the meat, but my mouth is bulging with it.

"I think you should listen to me on this matter, Peavey," Della says in grownup speak. So the kid won't know what they're talking about, which is okay, because I don't.

"I think I'm right, Ordella."

"Well, tell me something new!" Della's voice rises.

Peavey's head slides, and I realize he does that when he's

annoyed with her. "I asked for your advice, but it doesn't mean I have to take it."

He spits tobacco juice in his can. I gag. Seriously gag. The smoke from Della is fogging up the room. Their bickering is getting way old.

It makes me so mad. I want to yell at them to stop. I want to tell them to stay away from each other if all they're going to do is argue. I'd love to grab those newspapers off the floor and declare the house a tobacco-free environment.

And I almost do. I even stand up, but before anything comes from my mouth, I remember how Peavey treated me after I embarrassed him at the library. I think about how he let me mow so I wouldn't have to face him right away, then told me he'd been curious as a kid, too. How could I criticize a guy who was that good to me?

So I just walk outside and go back to work in the barn, letting them argue about God-knows-what in their smoky, cancer-producing world.

That afternoon I ask Peavey if he minds if I take a break. I've worked hard and I'm dirty and tired. He looks worn out, too.

"We'll all knock off a little early," he says. "Ronnie's got to get ready for the funeral, anyway."

Peavey and I go inside. I've been thinking about Della's roast for hours, so I cut off a slice, and sit down to watch Oprah. Peavey joins me. Today's show is about "unrequited love." She has several couples on the show. She brings out one person, listens to his or her lost-love story, then brings out the person he or she was in love with. You've got to won-der where she finds these people.

When I click it off, I look at Peavey and remember that he'd never had the courage to ask the woman he liked for a date.

"You know what this show reminds me of?" I ask. "It re-minds me of that story you told me about how you almost got married but never got to date her."

I'm trying to keep a straight face because this is impor-tant. Still, his thinking he was close to matrimony when he hadn't even kissed the girl makes me want to laugh.

"Hmm" is his only answer.

"Who was she?"

"Girl I knew."

"Did she move away?"

"Nope."

"Well, if you were on Oprah today, what would have been your story?"

He sits in silence. Sometimes I think Peavey's brain cogs are rusty and it takes a while for them to get moving.

"It was this time of year," he says. "The Sweet Corn Fes-tival."

I sit quietly so as not to disturb his thoughts.

"I'd been trying to get my courage up to ask her out and told myself it would be Saturday night of the festival. I sent a note with a friend saying I'd be waiting at Babbler's Knob."

"Where?" Then I bite my tongue for interrupting.

"It's a hill on the edge of town. It was a popular place for boys to take girls then. Kind of romantic, I guess you'd say."

"Did she show?" I ask.

"Yeah." He looks lost in thought. I try my best to keep quiet.

"Wore a blue dress and had a red rose stuck in her hair. Prettiest girl I'd ever seen." He smiles, shakes his head, and looks down.

"Well? What happened?"

"Right before I reached her, another fella came up and kissed her. That kiss knocked the flower out of her hair and the wind outa my sails." He gives me a half smile. "They left together. He got the girl and I got the flower. Kept that thing for years."

He slaps the arms of his recliner. "Well, enough of that."

He gets up and goes into the kitchen. I sit there for a minute thinking about how I feel when Erin is with Isaac. Peavey had to feel a whole lot worse.

I follow him into the kitchen. "You said she got married, right?"

"Is this going somewhere, Ed?" he asks, his tone suddenly cranky, which totally catches me off guard.

"I guess I wondered who she is."

"Doesn't matter now." He slices off some roast and begins warming beans in a pan.

"So she's still married," I push on.

"Nope."

"No?" Now we're getting somewhere.

"She was widowed," he says. "Now, that's enough. Are you gonna eat some more or are you through?"

"Um, I guess I'm through eating. But, Peavey, about this woman, why didn't you try again after she was widowed?"

"Once bitten, twice shy."

"So you were afraid to approach her again?"

"Ed, I've said all I'm gonna say on the subject."

I've learned that when Peavey says that, it's the God's honest truth. He leans against the sink, eating his roast and beans as I try to process what he just told me. Then a lightning bolt idea jolts through me on how to pay Peavey back for being nice about what I did at the library. Too bad Whip isn't here. I deserve to be called The Professor for this scheme, which is that I will try to get Peavey the woman he was in love with. But to pull it off, I'm going to need help. Most of all, I'll need help figuring out who this woman is.

When he finishes, I move to clean the kitchen, but Peavey says, "Leave it, Ed. I'd rather you go to the barn and make a list of what we have to do tomorrow."

"A list? Heck, I just do what you tell me to do. No way could I make a list on my own."

"Well, then, make sure we picked up everything so we can get a clean start in the morning."

"O . . . kay." I must have really ticked him off because it sounds like he just wants me out of the house. I go into the barn, but everything is put up, so I figure I'll toss the basketball until he gives me the all-clear to come back inside. Problem is, the ball is in my room. I decide to slip in, get it, then slip back out.

I see him still in the kitchen, so I go around and ease the

front door open. I'm just one step inside when I hear Peavey talking on the phone.

"Truth is, Lindy, Ordella and I have had quite an argument on whether or not to call you about it."

The blood freezes in my veins. He's talking to Mom about me.

"No, he doesn't suspect anything. Yes, I suppose I can drive him back. Well, yeah, it's true I'm busy this week with the festival. Are you sure you want him to come home?"

I'm breathing so hard I wonder why he doesn't look at me. Surely he hears me. I reach for the door and almost stagger outside.

He *said* he wasn't going to talk about it again.

He *said* he wouldn't tell Mom.

But he lied.

1 1

I take off down the street. At first I'm just wandering, unable to believe he called her, when he said he wouldn't. And here I was, about to help him get the woman he wanted. She doesn't know how lucky she is that she escaped being with him! Stupid tears come to my eyes and make me mad at myself for being such a baby and mad at him for causing them.

I pick up steam. I'm power-walking, pumping my legs and arms to burn off my anger. After a while, though, I realize I don't know where I am. I've never heard of the names I'm seeing on the street signs. At first I feel some panic, then realize everyone in Sheldon has to know everyone else. I'm sure anyone can help me get back to Peavey's—if I *want* to go back there.

I slow down, looking for someone to ask. I see a bunch of cars and head in that direction. I thought they might be at a store, but they're parked in a residential area. A crowd has gathered in a backyard, talking and eating off paper plates. Most of the people are dressed in black. A chill runs down my back and I start to cross the road to get away, until I remember that Mrs. Daly's funeral was today. Erin might be there. Even though I don't want her to matter anymore, she does.

I stand on the sidewalk in front of the house, trying to catch a glimpse of her, when I hear, "Hey, City!"

I flinch, feeling like I got caught stealing. Ronnie is sitting on the front porch and I didn't even see her. Not that I would have noticed her right away. Her hair is actually brushed and she has a skirt on. I'm not saying she looks *good*, but definitely more like a girl.

"What are you doing here?" She seems happy I'm here, which totally throws me.

I hesitate because I don't want to tell her I'm lost.

When I don't answer, she says, "Want some food? There's a ton in there."

I almost choke. Thinking about dying and food is enough to make you "go off your feed," as Della says.

"No, thanks," I say.

"We live next door." Ronnie tilts her head to the right. "I'm *that* close to home and can't go there."

"Too bad." I don't know what else to say.

"Come on, have a seat." She actually scoots over on the porch. I wonder if it's a trick, but decide to chance it. She's never been this nice before.

"Where were you headed?"

How can I tell her that Peavey betrayed me? She thinks the guy walks on water.

"I just thought I'd go for a walk." Ronnie nods, and I relax into the lie. "Check out the town, you know?"

"Wish I could go with you."

"You do?"

"Yeah, anything's better than this. Hey!" Her face brightens. "How about we find my mom and I'll introduce you. They'll think you're here for Mrs. Daly. I'll tell them you're new in town and need me to show you around! It's brilliant!"

I know this feeling. I've been here a hundred times with Whip. Just like him, Ronnie jumps up, grabs my arm, and pulls me toward the backyard. I wonder how I always end up with bossy people with bad ideas.

She stops in front of a dark-haired woman. "Mom? This is Eddie McCall. Peavey's nephew."

I shake her mom's hand, remembering that Peavey said she's a doctor. "Hi, Dr. Fielding."

"Very nice to meet you, Eddie." She smiles and, although she's older than my mom, I can tell she was pretty. Just like Erin.

"Eddie's new here and hasn't seen much of Sheldon. Would it be all right if I show him around?"

"Oh, honey. We really need to stay."

"Sheesh, Mom. Don't make Eddie feel bad for leaving."

"Veronica! I was talking about you, not Eddie." She looks embarrassed and I'd like to punch Ronnie, girl or not.

"It's okay," I say.

Before I can get another word out, a lady grabs my arm. "Micah, your mother is going to be upset that you took off your nice clothes. Better go change."

I jump, unsure of what's going on, but Dr. Fielding says, "Judith, this boy is Eddie McCall. Micah Daly is with his parents."

We both turn to where she is pointing. There stands Mr. Daly with a sad but polite look about him, sort of like an undertaker. Next to him is a woman who must be his wife and a kid with blond hair. He does look a little like a younger version of me.

The lady, Judith, releases the death grip on my arm.

"I'm so sorry," she says. "From across the lawn, you looked just like him."

She smooths her reddish hair that's pulled tightly into some kind of twist and smiles at me. "I guess I should start over. Given your resemblance to Micah, you must be related."

"I don't think so," I say.

"He's just leaving," Ronnie says, pushing me from behind.

I let her because eating food and having a party after burying someone is just not right.

"Wait!" Ronnie turns back, then kicks off her fancy shoes and gives them to her mother, leaving me standing by the food table.

I'm close enough to Mr. and Mrs. Daly that I hear them talking. He's murmuring to someone about how much he will miss his mother. When the person leaves, he turns to his wife and says, "I need a drink and I need it now."

Remembering what Peavey said about him, I listen in.

"Jeff, not now," his wife says. "It'll be over soon."

"Not soon enough," he says. "You know none of these people care. They're just being polite."

I decide this dude is seriously weird. I mean, what kind of person says something like that about his mom's funeral?

Ronnie comes back. "I'm ready."

I let her lead me through the crowd onto the sidewalk because my mind is stuck on what Mr. Daly said, wondering how a person can be such a phony. Then I think about how he talked to Erin and it gives me the creeps.

It's only then that I remember Erin. I didn't even get to see her.

Ronnie and I walk in silence. I don't think I should tell her what I overheard just now or how Mr. Daly acted with Erin. Instead I try to figure out why she's suddenly treating me as if I'm human instead of some two-headed alien, so I finally blurt out, "Okay, what's up? It's not like you to be nice to me."

She pulls a couple of leaves off a bush, holds one up, and says, "You." She lifts the other leaf. "Dalys." She lets the Daly leaf float away. "You're the lesser of two evils."

"I'll be sure to give you a call if I ever need a character witness."

She chuckles. "I should have gotten some money before leaving. I could use a soda. Do you have any?"

I shake my head. "It's at Peavey's and I'm not going back there."

She stops dead in her tracks. "City, say one bad thing about Peavey and I'll break your legs."

"Okay, number one, you sound like you've been watching old gangster movies. And, number two, haven't you ever just needed a break from the people you live with?"

She splits the leaf she's still holding into several strips, gives them a toss, and starts walking again. "Yeah."

"You know what I don't get?" I ask. "Why you're so mad all the time."

"I'm not mad all the time!"

"Most of the time you are. You call me 'City' like it's my fault I'm not from here. And why are you so protective of Peavey? I'm the kid that's staying with a strange man."

She sneers, and I can't help but compare that look to Erin's blinding smile.

"Wait," I say. "I meant he's basically a stranger to me, not that he's strange." Which isn't exactly what I meant, but it's what she wants to hear. Part of me knows this would be a good time to shut up, but I feel as if I'm going to bust with all the growing bad feelings I have for him.

"You know, Ronnie, Peavey isn't perfect."

She stops walking. "What are you saying?"

I stop, too. "I *said* what I'm saying."

"Nobody is perfect." She shoves my chest. "But he's a good man."

"You know what? I've had it with you pushing me around. And Peavey's not as good as you think." Then I do shut up, because what can I say? He broke his promise, it's true. But I'd have to tell her what I was looking at on the Internet, and I can't stand the thought of that.

"Really, City? You know him that well in less than two weeks? I've been around him my whole life, you jerk."

She runs past me toward a playground, then slides into a swing. I skip the one next to her and sit in the third one. She twists in the swing, and I can tell she's thinking.

"Peavey might not be perfect, but I can't take you saying anything negative after all he's done for you. Don't you feel at all guilty about the farm?"

Farm? "Uh, what are you talking about?"

She looks straight ahead, but she's talking to me. "That farm was all Peavey knew. When he heard about how *smart* you are"—she rolls her eyes as if that's hard to believe—"then he's all about selling his farm so he'll have the money to send you to college. He *said* he wanted to retire and open a lawn mower repair shop, but I think it was an act. I heard him tell Della the money your grandpa had put aside for you was used up with his illness."

I feel like I was plucked from planet Earth and dropped into a new galaxy.

"Not to sound stupid . . ." I say.

"Too late."

"Funny. What farm? And who told him I was smart? I've never heard about any of this."

"You never wondered why that big barn behind his house is right next to a convenience store? Or why his is the only *old* house in the neighborhood? He sold the land when your mom told him about you getting placed in advanced classes. Kelley's built on one side of him, and houses are springing up all around."

"I didn't know." My stomach tightens.

"And here's the thing that gets me." She pushes off and pumps her legs on the swing. "You act as if you smell something bad when you're around him. You probably live in a fancy apartment and attend some private school, and poor Peavey doesn't even have his farm anymore."

That's it. I slip out of the swing and walk away from her.

"Hey, wait a minute!" she calls. I keep walking, but she runs until she's caught up.

"What's your problem? Truth hurt?"

I take a deep breath and say, "My mom is single. She works *and* puts herself through school. Our apartment is so small she doesn't even have a bedroom. I have no idea who my old man is, so no help there. As for me being smart, other people decided that, not me. I never asked for college. It's just something my mom has mapped out for me."

"But you *seem* like a spoiled brat," she says.

"Really? As opposed to you, who always put others first?"

"I'd put Peavey before myself."

"I don't know anything about this farm. But, believe it or not, he's not as perfect as you think. And I'm talking about stuff you don't know anything about!"

She takes a step back. "Maybe," she says. "I just know he made a huge sacrifice for you."

"I don't *want* his farm money. You started this conversation, so tell me how to fix that. Can he buy his land back?"

"No. I told you, people are building on it."

"Will he take the money and buy himself something?"

"No, Peavey doesn't need much."

I press on. "Do I blame my grandpa for dying? Or my mom for telling him about my test scores? What do you want me to do here, Ronnie?"

"Just be nice to him!" she shouts at me.

"I have been!" I yell back. "I clean up after him. I help out as best I can in the barn. I'm trying!"

"Don't kid yourself, City," she says. "You're just marking time until you can go home."

She walks away and I let her go, because she's right. I can't wait to get away from him, especially now that I know what a liar he is.

I stay at the park, thinking, until dusk. Peavey had said that he and Della fought over whether or not to call Mom. That means he told Della, too. It's just as well he's taking me home. I'll never be able to face her again.

1 2

I find my way back to Peavey's, tell him I'm tired, and go to bed, but I don't sleep much. The next morning I feel as if I lost a fight. My head pounds when I stumble to the kitchen.

Peavey folds his newspaper and clears his throat. "Ed, uh, well, we need to talk."

I may have to go home today, but no one can force me to talk about it.

"We'll talk later, okay? I've got some stuff to do first."

I leave him sitting there. I try to remind myself that I should be thrilled. Who wants to be stuck in this backward town? Not me. I go into my room, make my bed, and pack my bags so they'll be ready. No sense in dragging it out when he admits that he turned me in to Mom and I have to go back home.

Ronnie is working when I get to the barn. I ignore her. She's already told me off, so what more can she say? The thought runs through my mind that if Peavey told my mom and Della, then he could have blabbed to Ronnie about the naked picture, too. Then I think, nah, even Peavey wouldn't do that.

I'm standing next to the bench when Ronnie comes over looking for a tool. I scoot away, but she gets closer still. Then she whispers, "I thought about our conversation last night. I was kind of hard on you. I mean, I had no idea you didn't know about the farm."

Oh, yes, Peavey's wonderful act of generosity. It had somehow gotten buried in my brain under all the mistrust. But I just say, "No problem."

She actually smiles at me, and I feel a sort of pang. Maybe it's gas. Or hunger. I didn't eat breakfast. But deep down I know it's neither. It's not leaving here that bothers me nearly as much as the way I'm leaving. Apparently Peavey's just going to tell me to get into his truck and whisk me out of here the same way he grabs up his muddy old newspapers off the floor.

If there's one good thing about overhearing him, it's knowing that I'm leaving. I'm not surprised when he says, "Ronnie, I know we've got a lot to do today, but I need to talk to Ed alone."

"So, talk! Who's stopping you?" She doesn't even raise her head from the engine she's working on.

"It's a private matter."

"Then go in the house. Peavey, I've been gone most of the week, and there's a lot of work to do, in case you haven't noticed."

"Ronnie." Peavey doesn't say anything else. It's a tone I've never heard before. Not yelling. Just firm.

"Okay, okay! I'm going! Just don't blame me when customers stop coming here."

She stomps over to Kelley's. I've been enjoying her attitude, but now I realize Peavey's going to come clean about calling my mom and I don't want to hear it.

"Don't say anything," I tell him. "I already know."

"How'd you find out?"

"It doesn't matter." I go into the house, pick up my gear, and throw it into the back of his truck.

"What are you doing?" he asks.

"You're getting rid of me," I say. "I heard you call Mom."

Peavey pulls down the tailgate of his truck and sits on it. "I wish you'd told me, Ed. Overhearing isn't how we wanted you to find out. Your mom and I just wanted to get you away from here before you put two and two together about Jeff Daly."

Now I'm confused. What in the world does Jeff Daly have to do with me? "But I'm talking about the library."

I hear him say, "The *library?*" but the words sound like they're coming from a distance because now other words he's said are bouncing around in my head. Words he said when I asked him about my dad . . . *Fathering a baby doesn't make a good dad* . . . and words about Mr. Daly . . . *Just because you're someone's dad doesn't make you a good man.*

I take a step back and put my hand on the tailgate to steady myself because I feel almost dizzy.

For some strange reason, a memory pops into my head of when I was younger and tried to figure stuff out while playing with Mom's Rubik's Cube. Right now I feel the same way I felt the first time the colors slid into their places.

All the greens are together: Mr. Daly's the father of Isaac and Micah, who look like me.

The yellows are together: Mom doesn't want me around Mr. Daly for a really good reason.

The blues are together: Mr. Daly is *my* father, too.

And the most important are the reds. And that thought is so scary that I have to ask. "Peavey, was Mr. Daly married to someone else? I mean, do all his kids have the same mom?"

Peavey nods with a sad look.

"But Isaac is older than I am and Micah and Leah are younger." And what I don't say out loud is that if that's true, then Mr. Daly got my mom pregnant with me while he was married.

He pats the tailgate. "Have a seat, Ed."

I shake my head and I don't remember moving, but somehow I'm sitting beside him.

"Lindy is the one who should be tellin' you this, but she's not here. Jeff was married when he fathered you."

I can't raise my eyes from the driveway. I feel that if I do, the ground might disappear from under me. It's like finding out everything I ever believed in isn't true. "There's no way"—I shake my head—"no way would I ever have thought my mom would mess around with a married guy."

"Now, hold on. It takes two, but you need to know the circumstances before you go judging her."

I hear him, but all I can think of is how I thought I knew my mom better than anyone and it turns out I don't know her at all.

"Your mom worked weekends at the Sheldon Hotel when she was a teenager. It was owned by the Dalys. Her mother had just died and it's easy to look back now and see how much Lindy was grieving. But at the time everybody was focused on Emery because his grief was so great. Lindy pretended to be strong for him."

"What does this have to do with anything?"

"I'm getting to that part," he says. "Jeff Daly was married, with a baby, but he was young. And he was her boss. She told us later that he helped her through that rough time of losing her mama."

I snort. "He sure did."

Peavey gives me a stern look until I turn away. "You've got the rest of your life to sort out your feelings. Now you have to hear the truth. Lindy came to Della when she found out she was pregnant. Della helped her tell your grandpa and me. It was important to Lindy to raise the baby on her own. She never told Jeff. Maybe she should have, maybe not. We all have difficult choices to make in life and she made hers.

"She finished school and your grandpa Emery set her up in an apartment in Chicago, where you were born. She's never been back to Sheldon."

Peavey takes off his hat and slaps his leg with it. "It's just like that ornery Arnetta Daly to die and bring in all the Daly kinfolk the one time you come for a visit."

I start to smile, but then I remember all the nasty things I've heard about Mrs. Daly and realize she's my relative.

"Ugh, that makes her my grandmother, doesn't it?"

"It doesn't matter now, does it? She's gone. Tell you what: you've had a lot of information for a fella to digest all at once. How about we take a break for lunch and if you want to talk more later, we can."

He tilts his head toward my suitcase. "You jumped the gun on going home, though. I was just gonna tell you that I was taking you home Saturday morning."

He grabs my bags from the truck bed and sets them on the ground. "Take these back inside, then run and tell Ronnie it's lunchtime."

I carry the bags inside, and lie back on the bed for a minute. Funny how this room doesn't seem creepy anymore. I want to just stay here and think about things, but I sit up because I've got to tell Ronnie we're taking lunch. Then I decide to splurge and buy my lunch at Kelley's so I can say goodbye to Erin. Heck, I'll even buy Ronnie's lunch, since she's already over there.

I walk into Kelley's, and Ronnie is sitting on a stool unwrapping a piece of gum. Erin is in the kitchen cutting a pizza. She bends over the counter as she works and I quickly look away.

"Are we going to work today or not?" Ronnie's sharp voice cuts into my thoughts.

"Yeah, but Peavey said to break for lunch. I thought I'd buy yours."

"For what? I can get my own lunch."

"Are you sure about that?"

Which causes her to say "Ooh!" She balls the gum wrapper and throws it at me. I laugh and pick it up. When I stand, Erin comes out of the kitchen. Despite myself, the sight of her still makes my legs almost buckle.

She goes to the front to wait on a customer, and I realize the customer is Isaac. Typical. Even when I come to say goodbye to Erin, her eyes are glued to my creepy half brother.

Then it gets worse. Mr. Daly comes in, too. I feel as if gravity has reversed itself and my weight is pounding into my head. He takes off his sunglasses, picks up a bottle of soda, and walks over to Erin and Isaac.

"That scuz next to Isaac is his dad," Ronnie whispers to me. I don't tell her I know darn good and well who he is.

She says louder to Erin, "Two cheese pizza slices for me and a large drink. Eddie's buying."

"Veronica, don't be rude. Mr. Daly and Isaac came to say goodbye."

Yes!

"So you're leaving, huh?" Ronnie says to *Mr. Daly*. I decide then and there I'm never going to call him anything but that.

"Yes, we've gotten lucky. Someone in town made an offer on the house, so we won't have to list it with a realtor. We'll come back for the closing in a month or so and pick up anything we want from the house then."

He hands Erin a twenty for the soda and says to Ronnie,

"I'm glad we have the chance to say goodbye to you, Veronica. I'm sorry you missed the rest of our family, though. They drove ahead."

Ronnie just nods and chews her gum. She's being kind of rude, but that's okay with me.

Erin counts out Mr. Daly's change, leaning across the counter a little. I could swear he looks down her shirt. I take a quick look at Erin and, sure enough, her shirt comes down to a "V" in the front. Not indecent or anything, but I'm sure from Mr. Daly's height he's getting an eyeful.

"Thank you, most beautiful Erin," he says.

She looks up, startled, and he's giving her a player face, half-closed eyes looking right at her with a trying-to-be-sexy smile. Erin's face turns bright pink.

I'm not the only one who sees it. Ronnie looks at me and makes a fake gagging sound. Isaac sees it, too, and just lets it happen. His own dad is flirting with a teenager. And not just any teenager, although that would be bad enough, but the daughter of a couple who have been helping him and his family.

Maybe Isaac's okay with it, but I'm not. I move and intentionally throw myself into the guy, knocking him sideways.

"Hey!" he says.

"Sorry," I say without even trying to sound sincere. "That's the second time today I've tripped."

"S'okay," he says, brushing at his clothes.

"Well, we don't want to keep you." I step to the side so he can pass.

He gathers the bills Erin was giving him and tucks them into his wallet, then looks at me. He frowns. "Have we met?"

"This is Eddie McCall," Ronnie says, and I can tell by the way she says it that she enjoyed my move.

"McCall? I used to know a Linda McCall from here. Are you related?"

My stomach cramps at him saying my mother's name.

"That's his mom," Ronnie says. "Right, Eddie?"

I nod. He squints at me hard, really checking me out. He looks into my eyes, and I match him stare for stare.

He has a look of recognition on his face. Or maybe it's dread. "You say your name is McCall. That was Linda's maiden name."

I get how important my answer is. Peavey talked about making choices, and it hits me that I have a crucial choice to make here. It's true I've always wanted a dad, but I do not want this man for my father. So I glare into the blue eyes that look exactly like the ones I see in the mirror every morning and I lie.

"Yes, my mom kept her maiden name when she married. That's pretty common."

He looks away, obviously thinking. "How old are you?"

I do some quick math. "I just turned twelve last month." The truth is, I turned thirteen three months ago.

"Really, Eddie?" Erin says. "I thought you were older."

"He just seems older, right, Eddie?" Ronnie says. I don't know why she's helping me, but I'm grateful for it.

"I take after my dad." The lies come easier. Mr. Daly

looks a little over six feet tall, so I say, "He's six foot six. You'll see when he picks me up at the end of the month."

Mr. Daly's frown lifts. The guy lets out a shaky breath and smiles. You can almost see relief oozing from his slimy pores.

Ronnie speaks up. "Erin, why don't you give us our food. We're in a hurry and you guys want to say goodbye."

She's got that right. I *am* in a hurry. To get away from that man.

I pay Erin and somehow get out of Kelley's, but it's as if I'm walking underwater—moving slowly and not hearing or seeing well. I don't even try to look back. All I can think is that when I finally meet my father, he turns out to be scum.

I follow Ronnie back to the barn. She clears space at the workbench and sets out our food. There is something about the familiarity of the barn and Ronnie's calm attitude that allows me to feel as if I've broken the surface again.

"Why didn't you say anything?" I ask her. "You knew I was lying."

"I figured you had your reasons." She bites into the pizza. "Be careful. It's hot."

We eat and she doesn't say another word about what happened. She looks a mess. She's wearing coveralls and has a grease streak across her cheek. But I could hug her for not asking any questions. And even though I should tell her I'm leaving this weekend, I just can't.

I can't help thinking about how Mr. Daly looked at Erin. Then I think about what I did on the Internet and I realize it wasn't so different—except of course I'm not an older, married man. But still.

Peavey comes back out after lunch. I see his step-swing, loping walk and I just have to talk to him. I look at Ronnie and slurp the last of my Coke. "I sure wish we'd bought two of these each. It's pretty hot out today."

"You buy and I'll fly," she says, just like I hoped she would. I hand her a couple of bills. She hops off her seat and swaggers over toward Kelley's.

"Where's she off to?"

"I needed to talk to you for a minute."

"Okay." Peavey sits on the stool Ronnie just vacated. "Shoot."

"It's about the library," I say.

"You mentioned that earlier. What about the library?"

"I thought that's what you called my mom about. You know . . . what I did there."

"I gave you my word, Ed," he says. "It never crossed my mind to tell anyone."

"Still, Peavey." I look at him. "What I did there, it makes me like Mr. Daly . . . like my dad, right? A pervert?"

"Well, let's have a look." He jumps off the stool, pulling me with him. He looks up at me. "You've got his height. Trust me, coming from a family of runts, that's a good thing."

Peavey walks around me like he's looking a horse over to buy. "You look a mite like his boys, but not so much like him. You've got enough of Lindy in you to keep you from bein' ugly."

I know he's teasing, but I'm not in the mood.

"I don't mean how I look. When you talked about Isaac, you said, 'the apple doesn't fall far from the tree.' Isn't that true for me, too?"

"Let me finish." He stops in front of me. "As I recall, Jeff Daly graduated near the top of his class, so I'd say you've got his smarts. He was also good in sports, and I've seen you toss that basketball around. You probably got that from him, too."

"I don't want anything from him."

"Now, Ed, you don't want to thump a free melon. Not everyone is all bad. I'd say you've picked up a few good genes from him."

"What about the bad, Peavey? That's what scares me."

"The bad. Well, now, that's more of a choice, I think. No one held a gun to his head. He made the choice to take advantage of Lindy. From what you said about Erin, sounds like he'd do it again. You know it's wrong, and you're not even shaving yet. Nope, I can't see you making the same choices."

"But I already did, right? I mean, I downloaded that stuff at the library. No one held a gun to my head, either."

"True enough. You were curious. Now you'll have to be the one to decide if you'll do it again."

I can't say I feel good now, but I know I'd feel a lot worse if it weren't for what Peavey just said.

Ronnie comes back, thrusts a pop at me, and tells Peavey that all the Dalys are gone.

"Now things can get back to normal around here," she says.

He looks at me with his eyebrows raised in an unspoken question.

I nod, and he nods back. Nothing else needs to be said.

13

We work hard for the rest of the day, then get up early on Friday to finish tuning up the last of the parade tractors. We don't talk much. Still, I see by the way Ronnie relaxes around me that she notices I'm nice to Peavey. Really nice, that is, not just polite.

Finally the last of the tractors is done and Peavey tells us to knock off for the day.

"I reckon you two will want to go downtown now and see the sights."

"No, not if the 'sights' include people worshiping a vegetable."

Ronnie thumps me on the back of the head. "No, not if the 'sights' include being seen with you, City."

She swaggers off and I go into the house.

"You messed up," Peavey says when he comes in. "You go back home in the morning and tonight could have been a fun last night here. I know this festival is small potatoes to you, but it's still a good time." He stares out the window for a bit, but when he turns back, there is a lost look in his eyes. I think it's because I'm leaving, but then he says in kind of a sad voice, "Yessir, it sure can be a good time."

Then I remember it was at the festival that he lost the girl he loved. I'd been so wrapped up in my own problems, I totally forgot that I wanted to try to get them back together. But I don't know who she is. Much as I hate to admit it, I could use Ronnie's help.

"Peavey, I've changed my mind. I think I'll see if Ronnie will go to the festival with me."

"In that case, I'll send money for your supper."

"I've got money," I say. I don't have much after buying yesterday's lunch, but I don't want to take his money.

"No arguing. It was a bad week for you to start helping me, with the festival coming up, and Ronnie always works her tail off. My treat."

He shoves a wad of bills into my hand.

"I can't take that!"

"Consider it pay," he says. "Half is Ronnie's. You've both worked hard this week. There'll be lots of vendors in town and you'll need spending money. Go on now."

I take a quick shower, then head toward Ronnie's house. I get there and knock on the door. After a while, she answers. She's taken a bath. Her hair is still wet and she has clean clothes on. They aren't girly clothes, but they're not boys' clothes, either. I think about telling her she should wear them more often, but don't.

"What's up, City?" she says.

"Have you got a minute?"

"Yeah, I guess." She comes outside.

"I need your help." I tell her Peavey's story. When I finish, I say, "So she lives here in town and she's widowed. I think it would be pretty cool to help him try and get her back."

"I had no idea," she says.

"Do you want to help?" I ask.

"I'd do anything for Peavey. But how do you know he still wants her?"

"Duh. He kept her stupid flower for years. What do you think? We've got to figure out who she is."

Ronnie shakes her head. "It's just that he's never told me any of this. And he keeps to himself. As much as I'd like to help, I think it's impossible."

Then she looks at me. "I have to admit, I didn't figure you to be a romantic."

"I'm not!" I say, my face hot. "I was just tryin' to help the guy, that's all. I mean, all these years and he obviously can't do it himself. Just forget it."

I get up to leave, but she says, "Wait, I think it's nice of you."

When I don't say anything, she adds, "Really."

"Oh." I stick my hands in my pockets for something to do and feel Peavey's money. "Hey, I almost forgot. Peavey sent some money. He wants us to go to the festival."

She looks at me like she's sizing me up.

"Look, if you don't want to . . ."

"Don't be so touchy," she says. "I want to. Let's go get something to eat. I'm starved."

We head into town.

The first food vendor we find is selling corn dogs. I order two each, but Ronnie says, "Make that one each. There's a lot of food. We'll want to taste it all."

We add mustard and walk down the crowded street. I didn't know there were that many people living in Sheldon. But then I've only met a few. Most have been friendly, even that nut-job Louise.

I stop suddenly and throw out my arm to stop Ronnie, too. Unfortunately, it's the one holding the corn dog.

"Watch it!" she says, dabbing her mustard-smeared shirt.

"Sorry!" I say. "But I just figured out who Peavey's woman is. She's been hot over him since I got here."

"Hot? Over Peavey! Nah."

"Seriously."

"Who?"

"Louise."

As we walk down Main Street eating the corn dogs, I think I'm starting to understand the people of Sheldon. It isn't that they like corn so much. They just want an excuse to have fun.

Ronnie and I keep going over the problem of Louise. One of us will have to talk to her, and I don't know her at all. Ronnie says she doesn't know her well enough. "Besides," she says, "Louise seems peculiar to me."

I start to say "A match made in heaven," but don't. Peavey may be a little peculiar, but not in a bad way like I thought.

Instead I say, "It'd be great to do it this weekend. I mean, he wanted to ask her out at the Sweet Corn Festival before."

"I know, *City*." Emphasis on my name, which tells me I'm getting on her nerves.

"Well, at least you know Louise a little. I don't know her at all."

We walk on, both lost in thought.

We come to carnival booths, a dunking tank, and crafts for sale. There's a long flatbed trailer that Ronnie says is used as a stage for entertainment and the Miss Sweet Corn Queen contest. I almost laugh over that one, until she tells me that Erin won two years ago. Then I think of my mom. For all I know, she might have been a corn queen herself at one time. She probably would love this festival, since she grew up here.

But she's stuck at home. And worse, she's alone, thanks to me. If I hadn't acted like I did, she would at least have Whip's company. I might not be able to do anything about her not being here, but I can do something about her being alone.

"Let's find a phone."

I feel to see if I crammed my calling card into the pocket with the money, then look up at Ronnie holding a cell phone out to me.

"Am I the only kid in the world without one of those things?" I ask.

"Technically, it's our 'family' phone. My folks call the

spares that because they don't want Erin or me to feel privileged."

"Do you?" I ask. "Feel privileged?"

She snorts. "I'd rather not have the phone and have a parent around once in a while. Why do you think I hang out at Peavey's so much?"

"Because you're a tomboy," I want to say, but right now she doesn't look so much like one. I don't know what she's done, other than take a bath, but something's different.

"Well, thanks." I punch in Whip's number.

"Yo!" he says.

"Whip, it's Eddie."

"Don't know anyone by that name. Guess you got the wrong number."

"Don't hang up!" I move away from Ronnie so she won't hear.

"I need a favor and before you say no it's for my mom."

He's silent for about five seconds, then says, "So? What's the favor?"

"Spend some time with her tonight, okay? I was kind of a jerk before."

"Kind of?"

"Okay, a huge jerk. I've thought it over and I'm glad she likes you and you like her. Now go keep her company."

"I'll never get past the door. She doesn't want to upset her little baby boy."

Wow, he really is mad. "Then tell her this, tell her I sent you and tell her something else. Say, ahoy matey."

"What the—"

"Just do it!" I click off before he can say anything else.

Feeling about fifty pounds of guilt lighter, I say, "Now, any ideas for Peavey and Louise?"

"No. It doesn't have to be this weekend, you know," Ronnie says. "You'll be here for a few more weeks."

But I won't be here after today, and for some reason I still can't say the words.

"It should be today," I say. "Trust me."

We walk along and see what looks like a horse trough, only it's way bigger. Guys are filling it with water and Della is there.

I tap Ronnie on the arm and we run over to her.

"Hey, Della!" I say.

"Hey, yourself!"

Her shirt says SHELDON, PUTTING THE SWEET IN CORN. It wouldn't be so bad, but "sweet" is in really big letters and it falls right over her tummy bulge. I concentrate on her face.

"What are you doing?" I ask.

"Stick around and you'll see. This will be full of the best ears of corn you've ever tasted and it's all you can eat for free."

"Wow," I say, knowing a part of me will always think their enthusiasm for their veggies is a little extreme.

"Did Peavey come with you?" she asks.

"No, you know Peavey," Ronnie says, then hits her forehead. "Della! You *do* know Peavey."

Della laughs. "Oh, honey, I know Peavey! Why, I can see through that man like a lace curtain."

I get where Ronnie is going with this. "And you probably know Louise, right?"

"Louise Murray? Sure. What about her?"

"Well, Peavey . . ." Ronnie looks at me.

"Peavey takes care of her," I say. "He mows for her and looks out for her."

Della nods. "Yes. She used to write him when he was sick with polio. He never forgot that."

"That's nice," I say.

"She's a kooky old flirt," Della says. "But harmless."

"Yeah, well, we think Peavey more than likes her and we want to get them together. Maybe you can help us."

Della fumbles for her cigarettes and motions us to the picnic tables set up nearby.

"Now, what's this about him and Louise?" She lights her cigarette.

I ignore the smoke since we're outdoors, but I do sit up-wind. "He told me he was in love with a girl. I mean he didn't use the word *love* but he wanted to marry her so I guess he was. Anyway, he sent her a note on the Saturday of the Sweet Corn Festival, and she ran off with some other guy."

Della shakes her head, obviously confused. "Did he tell you anything else?"

I think real hard. "Yeah, he sent a note asking her to meet him at Babbler's Knob and she had on a blue dress with a red rose in her hair. Before he could reach her, some other guy came up to her and kissed her. Then they went off together."

"Oh, don't forget the flower," Ronnie said. "Her rose fell

out and he kept it for years, so it had to be really serious. But we don't know Louise or how to approach her. She *is* kind of odd and all."

Della stands up really quick. "I've got to get the corn on," she says. "But I'll think on it."

She leaves her cigarette on the table. I flip it onto the ground and stomp on it.

14

I get up early Saturday morning. Peavey is dressed and waiting to take me home.

"Best get your bags," he says. "Your mom is expecting us around noon."

I lay awake last night thinking about my newfound gene pool. Living with Peavey this past week has made me realize how much he's done for my mom and me. I may have Jeff Daly in me, but I know I'm related to Peavey McCall, too. Peavey might be a little odd, but he's got his priorities straight.

"Hey, remember how you told me you'd teach me the stuff a guy should know, like fixing a lawn mower? How am I supposed to learn anything if you send me home?"

"Now hold on, Ed. It's not that I want you to go."

"Then don't make me. Call my mom and talk her into letting me stay. Now that I know who my father is, there's no rush, right?"

"Well . . ."

"So call her and tell her I want to stay the rest of my break."

That too-much-gum grin breaks out on his face, but it's nice to see. It tells me he wants me to stay.

"Don't you think you should tell her that yourself?" he says.

I was afraid of that. I know I need to talk to her; I'm just not quite ready yet. "Tell her I'll call her later. Right now I need to meet Ronnie."

"Okay, it's a deal."

As I head out the door, Peavey says, "Oh, and Ed? Glad you're stayin'."

I nod. Nothing else needs to be said. I'm learning from him already.

When I get to Ronnie's house, she's waiting on the porch with a box of doughnuts and two glasses of milk, which is really nice. In other words, it's totally not Ronnie. She looks good again today, not Stormy good or Erin good, but still. I sit down and get a whiff of perfume. It's not what Erin uses, but it's nice in its own way—like Ronnie, I guess.

When we're done, she wads up the trash, runs it inside, and comes back out. "Let's find Della."

Turns out we don't have to look far. Della is pacing and smoking in front of the same picnic table as last night. The giant corn trough is clean and ready for another day. She sees us and pulls out an envelope with Peavey's name on it.

I take the envelope. It's sealed tight. "You talked to her?"

"All taken care of," she says.

"Do you know what's in it?" Ronnie asks.

"It says to be at Babbler's Knob at seven," Della says. "I'd advise you not to be there when he reads it. He's a private man."

"Do you think he'll come?" Ronnie asks.

Della shrugs. "It's been a long time and he got stood up, honey. But I hope so."

Ronnie and I go back to the house. We see Peavey out in the barn, so we tape the envelope to the refrigerator door, where he'll see it at lunchtime. Now that Della knows about the plan, I'm in a much better mood and ready to have fun. I can tell Ronnie is, too.

We hit town again to watch the parade. The corn queen waves from the first float. All the tractors look nice and clean, and I actually feel a little proud of the work we did on them. After the crazy clowns go by in their bathtub cars and on their little bikes, Ronnie and I move on.

At one point I see Joseph from the library. I'd like to hide, but when Joseph sees me, he yells, "Hey, Eddie! Just got a new order of graphic novels in. You need to come by next week."

I cannot believe the relief I feel. Joseph and Peavey are both giving me a second chance.

Ronnie and I move through the crowd. We eat elephant ears, these really big, flat pieces of dough that are deep-fried and have sweet stuff on them. Then we eat lunch at another booth. As the afternoon wears on, we check the time. We've planned to hide near Babbler's Knob to watch Peavey and Louise. Some might call it stalking. I prefer to think of it as our reward for getting them together.

We play a few carnival booths. Ronnie tosses Ping-Pong balls into fishbowls and wins a goldfish, which she gives to a little kid.

"That was easy," I say. "Let's move on to something harder."

"Oh, listen to the big guy. Easy, huh? Pick something tougher and show me up, then."

Little does Ronnie know how many basketball games Whip and I have played. I go to the hoops booth, line up, and make six free throws in a row—enough to win a stuffed animal, which neither of us wants. Still, I feel good.

"Not bad, Eddie."

"Ronnie, I hate to break it to you, but you just called me Eddie."

"And?" she says.

"And you call me City. 'Eddie' sounds almost as if you like me."

"Maybe you're not so dumb, after all," she says.

Is she saying what I think she's saying? I look at her. She doesn't look away, but slowly smiles, and there it is. Whether I want to admit it or not, I know that deep down I really like being with Ronnie. She's a pain, sure, and not all feminine and flirty like Erin, but still.

I wonder what Whip would think of Ronnie, and I'm kind of glad he's not here to steal her attention. Then I start thinking about him and wonder if he visited my mom.

"Can I use your cell?" I ask.

"I don't have it on me," she says.

"Jeez, the one time I expect to use one and there isn't any. I need to make a call and I don't want to run into Peavey."

"We'll go to my house."

We do. I wait in the living room. It's pretty nice, about the nicest room I've ever been in. Everything is light gold and makes you want to take a bath before sitting down.

I walk over to the piano and look at the pictures propped on it. Ronnie comes back just as I'm noticing one of her playing the flute.

"I didn't know you were musical," I say.

"I'm not."

"Then why are you playing the flute in this picture?"

"That's Erin," she says. "She was in eighth grade."

I squint at it and I swear I can't tell any difference between eighth-grade Erin and Ronnie today. I know that I like Ronnie anyway, but thinking that she might look like Erin someday—well, a guy can think about these things.

She hands me a portable phone and leaves to give me some privacy. I dial Mom; she sounds really happy.

"Peavey said you'd call later, but I wasn't sure. This is the first call I've gotten from you since you left."

"I wanted to check if Whip's been around. I mean, I told him to."

"Yes, he has. He and his dad took me out for Chinese last night, which was really sweet of them."

"Well, good. I'm glad he came over." I clear my throat. "Mom, I want to stay in Sheldon for the rest of my break."

"You do?"

"Well, yeah. I mean, now that I know who my *father* is, there's no rush, right?" I don't like that my voice is coming out all hurt sounding, but I can't help it.

Mom probably doesn't like the sound of her voice, either. It's shaky as she says, "Honey, we should have talked about it a long time ago. I'm so sorry you found out this way. So you've . . . met him."

"Yeah."

"Oh, God," she says. "Eddie, he never knew about you."

"Yeah, I figured that out. I have a feeling he suspected who I was, but I threw him off with a few lies."

"And I'm sure he grabbed onto them." She sighs loudly.

"Yeah, he's a real stand-up guy."

"Eddie, there's no excuse for my behavior, but my mother had just died and I'd never felt so alone in my life. Jeff was my boss at the hotel."

"No wonder you're taking classes to get away from hotel work," I say.

She laughs and it kind of breaks the ice. She sounds more like the Mom I know.

"We were close in age and I was comfortable talking to him. And he encouraged it."

I thought about how he looked at Erin. "I'll bet he did."

"I didn't want to break up his marriage. I didn't want *anything* from him, so I never told him about you. I'm ashamed of how it happened, but, Eddie, you need to know this: I've always been proud to be your mother."

"Except when I do stuff like that Internet thing."

"You mean the thing that I overreacted to? I've done a lot of talking with Sam about that, and we both realize there's a happy medium."

"Sam? Mr. Sweeney?" It just hits me that she said he and Whip took her out for Chinese food. "Are we talking about the same guy you said is 'irresponsible' and has 'commitment issues'? The one whose child 'lacks supervision'?"

"Oh, that."

Yeah, that. As much as I like Mr. Sweeney, I wonder if my mom is a loser magnet when it comes to choosing guys.

"Do you remember those women I thought were Sam's girlfriends?"

"Uh-huh."

"They're Whip's tutors."

"No way!"

"Yes, Eddie. He works really hard for his grades. He's not lucky like you."

"Whip never told me."

"Anyway, Sam and I asked Whip for your passwords and we closed out both your e-mail accounts. Not to be mean, but to keep you safe. We're starting new ones for you two with passwords that we'll know and will be checking. But you'll have e-mail and the use of the computer—with parental controls—when you get home."

"Yes!"

She laughs. We say goodbye, and I find Ronnie to give her back the phone.

"It's about time to go, Eddie," Ronnie says. "It's getting close to seven. Louise should be there."

159

Louise. Something dawns on me. "Ronnie! Peavey always gives people he cares about a nickname!"

"Yeah? So?"

"But Louise! He calls her by her name!"

"Oh, jeez!" she says. "It's not her, is it?"

"I don't think so."

"We've got to stop him."

We run out the door, with Ronnie leading the way. The streets are full of people because some mud-hopping, clog-stomping, something-or-other dancers are performing. We race past the stage and Ronnie shoots down a side street. I do my best to keep up.

"Would you hurry!" she calls over her shoulder.

"I'm trying!"

Ronnie never slows down. She weaves in and out of streets. Finally we're on the outskirts of town and she heads across a field, slowing us both down.

"Stop!" I'm panting. "If we're too late, we don't want him to see us. He'll die of embarrassment."

"I *know*! You think I don't know that?" she yells.

"I'm just *saying*!"

"Well, you don't have to. Just follow me."

Finally I see an old, run-down shed. Ronnie crouches and gets behind it. I crouch down, too. We're too late. I can see the back of Louise's gray head and her blue dress. Peavey's truck is already there, and he gets out. He's wearing a suit, necktie and all. Carrying a hat, he walks up to her.

There's nothing for us to do but let it happen. I know we shouldn't watch, but I can't move.

Peavey whistles his stupid one-note. I cringe, thinking he's going to blow this. She turns around. Ronnie grabs my arm, her eyes huge because it's not Louise at all. It's Della in a blue dress with a red rose tucked behind her ear. I've never seen her with anything but her T-shirts on. She looks kind of nice for an old lady.

"I'm a little nervous," I hear her say to Peavey. "Mainly because I'm not smoking."

Peavey ducks his head. "I gave up the chew, too."

"Sorry I'm a few years late, Peavey."

"I guess I should have signed my name on the note."

"That might have helped." She laughs a nervous-sounding laugh. Then she gets serious. "I thought it was from Arthur."

Peavey bobs his head a few times like he's agreeing. "I sent the note with him."

"Why didn't you ever say anything, Peavey? And you stayed a true friend to him all those years after he did that."

"I figured he must really love you to come and get you before me. Besides"—Peavey looks at the ground—"maybe you'da never come if you'd known it was me."

"I'd have come. I'm here now, aren't I?"

She takes a step toward him.

He holds out his hand to her.

Ronnie yanks me backward.

"Hey!" I whisper.

"It feels weird watching now."

"I know. Like it's too private."

Then we look at each other and smile.

161

"It worked," she says.

I nod. "It looks like Peavey's days of putting down newspapers are over."

We sit with our backs against the shed. She shakes her head. "I just don't get it. They act as if they don't like each other at all."

"Yeah," I say. "I mean, they fight all the time."

We look at each other and then both look away really fast.

"It's time for the free corn," she says, like that's something we care about.

"Free corn?" I play along. "We can't miss that."

We head back to town, not touching, but close. Every three or four steps, our hands brush. Ronnie doesn't pull away, just walks close enough to let it happen, which makes me feel as if a party is going on in the pit of my stomach. It's not that scared-but-excited feeling from the stuff on the Internet, and it's not the nervous-breathless feeling of visiting Erin at Kelley's.

It's better.